SUMMER OF WEDDINGS

Claire loves her job as a teacher, but always looks forward to the long summer break when she can head out into the world in search of new adventures. However, this summer is different. This summer is full of weddings. When Claire meets Gabe, a handsome American in a black leather jacket and motorbike boots, on the way to her best friend Lorna's do, she wonders if this will be her most adventurous summer yet. Will the relationship end in heartache, or a whole new world of possibilities?

SPECIAL MESSAGE TO READERS

THE ULVERSCROFT FOUNDATION
(registered UK charity number 264873)

was established in 1972 to provide funds for research, diagnosis and treatment of eye diseases. Examples of major projects funded by the Ulverscroft Foundation are:-

- The Children's Eye Unit at Moorfields Eye Hospital, London
- The Ulverscroft Children's Eye Unit at Great Ormond Street Hospital for Sick Children
- Funding research into eye diseases and treatment at the Department of Ophthalmology, University of Leicester
- The Ulverscroft Vision Research Group, Institute of Child Health
- Twin operating theatres at the Western Ophthalmic Hospital, London
- The Chair of Ophthalmology at the Royal Australian College of Ophthalmologists

You can help further the work of the Foundation by making a donation or leaving a legacy. Every contribution is gratefully received. If you would like to help support the Foundation or require further information, please contact:

**THE ULVERSCROFT FOUNDATION
The Green, Bradgate Road, Anstey
Leicester LE7 7FU, England
Tel: (0116) 236 4325**

website: www.ulverscroft-foundation.org.uk

SARAH PURDUE

SUMMER OF WEDDINGS

Complete and Unabridged

LINFORD
Leicester

First published in Great Britain in 2019

First Linford Edition
published 2020

A catalogue record for this book is available
from the British Library.

ISBN 978–1–4448–4575–4

Young, Free – and Single

Claire loved receiving post as a child. She loved to hear the postman's boots crunch up the gravel drive and then the clang of the letterbox, followed by the soft thud of letters and postcards landing on the mat. Then there was the excitement of racing to be the first to collect them up and discover if there were any postcards from Grandma and Grandad.

But this spring, she had begun to dread walking into her flat and checking her small box in the row of post boxes on the wall of the high ceilinged hall. The sun was playing through the stained glass front door as she looked at her box which seemed to be so full that she could see at least two envelopes sticking out of the bottom of the door.

There had been a time, not too many

months ago, when she didn't even need to check it every day. Nobody wrote her letters any more and all her bills came electronically so usually all she had to do was clear out and recycle the inevitable junk mail. But now it seemed it was wedding invitation season and all of her friends past and present seemed to be getting married.

Claire had known it was coming. Several friends had sent out 'save the date' cards but since those had arrived more than a year in advance of the dates, Claire hadn't thought too much about it. It was only last week, when she sat down and started to enter all the dates into her diary, that she realised the scale of this year's wedding season. All but one of the summer weekends now had a wedding in it.

Claire pushed her key into the lock of her post box and turned it. It wasn't easy to open the door, since one letter had slipped through the side and was now preventing her from opening the box door fully. With a sigh and a silent wish, she tugged that envelope free and then pulled out the rest and dumped them into her bag.

Mrs Jacobs, who lived in the downstairs flat, breezed through the front door with her entourage of tiny dogs skipping in her wake.

'Claire, dear, how are you today?'

'I'm fine, Mrs Jacobs, thank you.'

'You look tired. It's all those hours that you put in at school. I hope the parents appreciate all your hard work.'

Claire smiled.

'I'm sure they do.' Although Claire could think of one mother who did nothing but complain about everything to do with her son, who she believed was an absolute angel, which was not quite how Claire would describe him.

Thinking of the school reports and marking that she had in one of her large supermarket reusable bags, Claire headed towards the stairs. She was very fond of Mrs Jacobs but if Claire didn't make a move she would be invited in for a cup of tea and a slice of delicious cake which would not be in the best interest of either her marking or the outfits she was going to wear during the summer of weddings.

'I've more work to do, so I'd best be getting on.'

'Of course you do and don't let me keep you. Just let me know if you fancy a slice of cake and I'll have Charles run it up to you.'

Claire smiled and made her way up the wooden staircase that would take her up to her flat. Her flat was part of an old Victorian mansion house that had been converted. Mr and Mrs Jacobs and their tribe of small dogs lived downstairs and they owned the long garden out the back. The first floor flat was owned by a young couple and Claire's own flat was on the second floor. She might not have had a garden but what she did have was a glorious view of west London from her Juliet balcony that she wouldn't swap for the world.

Claire liked nothing better than

kicking off her shoes after work, pulling open the balcony doors and moving her chair so that she could sit, book in one hand and chilled glass of rosé in the other, with her feet resting on the metal guard and looking out over the city which had become her home.

But not tonight, she thought, as she pushed her key into the keyhole and unlocked the door. Tonight she needed to write school reports and mark the science work that her nine-year-olds had completed the day before, and once she had done that, well then she could relax.

Claire took off her work shoes and slid out of her suit jacket which she hung on the wall mounted coat stand. She dragged the bags with her and threw them on to the small, rather saggy sofa and as she did so, the pile of envelopes escaped and spilled over the floor. Splayed out, there seemed to be even more than there had been in her post box. Some of the envelopes had a pearlised sheen and some were bright white but all spoke of heavy weight paper and their own importance.

She flicked the switch on the kettle and moved into her bedroom to change out of her work clothes and into her yoga trousers and a baggy top. She might have to work but she could at least be comfortable.

Once changed she made a cup of tea and selected a ready meal from her freezer stock. None of them was particularly appealing but she knew she didn't have time to cook, let alone go out and shop for ingredients.

Moving back to the sofa, she pulled her work issue laptop from its carrying case and clicked it on, waiting for the ancient beast to warm up. She stacked the children's reports in one pile and their science reports in another.

Despite this time wasting technique, her computer was still a blank screen with a slowly rotating egg timer and so she knew that she couldn't put it off any longer. The envelopes were where she had left them, fanned out on the slightly threadbare carpet and she needed to open them. Before she did, she got out her diary and opened it to the first weekend of the school summer holidays.

Claire opened the first envelope, a pale lilac, and read the invitation. It was from Steve, a friend she had met during her teacher training course, or more likely from Kim, his wife-to-be. Claire flicked through to the third weekend of the summer holidays and updated the details for the wedding, before setting the invitation aside and picking up the next envelope.

It was nearly an hour later when Claire had opened all the envelopes and the fact was staring her in the face. It was true. She now had a wedding booked into every weekend of her precious six week summer holidays.

With a sigh, she flopped back on to the sofa. It wasn't that she didn't like weddings, she loved them and she loved her friends. It was just that the six week holidays represented freedom for Claire. Each year Claire worked through every holiday so that she could take some time off in the summer and head off for an adventure. And foreign adventures wouldn't be easy to come by if she needed to be at a different location in the UK every weekend.

It would be great to meet up with her friends, of course. Claire had moved to London and her friends from university had spread out across the UK, but mainly in the north of the country and so it was difficult for the close-knit group to all meet up at the same time. And since her friends were all teachers, it wasn't a particular surprise that they were booking their weddings in for the long summer break, it was more of a surprise that they had all chosen the same summer to get married.

Claire leaned forward and picked up her diary. With weddings spread out across the UK, maybe that would be this year's adventure. She wouldn't be flying off to an exotic location but surely there would be adventures to be had in the UK? And it would be great to meet up with everyone.

Not everyone would be at every wedding, since some of the couples would surely be on honeymoon, but for Claire it would be an opportunity to spend some quality time with her friends. She missed them.

Maybe staying home would be good for her? One thing was for sure, with all those outfits and wedding presents to buy, she wouldn't have a problem finding a use for her hard earned holiday savings.

Claire put aside her diary and picked up the laptop, which had warmed up and then gone back to sleep. She needed to get on with some work or she would be burning the midnight oil and then getting up at six to go back to work.

She started to write the first school report, for Maisie Jones, a bright and sweet girl who reminded Claire why she had chosen to teach. The words came easily. There was a lot of good to say about young Maisie but even that could not distract Claire from the real issue that was bothering her. It had nothing to do with giving up all her weekends in her holidays, or the money she would be spending. No, it all came down to one thing. Once again, for six weeks, Claire would be going to a series of events all by herself.

Her friends were pretty much all in couples now. In fact it seemed like they were all getting married, but it was the same now as it had been back at uni. Claire was single and any single person knows that the event most likely to remind you of the fact that nobody wanted to marry you, was other people's weddings.

Two's Company

Claire was at the airport. Since it was the day after the last day of term, it was heaving. Everywhere she looked, there were queues. Queues of people, every age and culture, but all with two things in common: they carried or pulled heavy suitcases and they were all waiting. Waiting to check in their heavy bags.

Claire was glad that she had decided to go a different route and take only a carry on. This had been helped somewhat by the choice of wedding outfit. For this first wedding, Claire was the maid of honour.

Her best friend Lorna had travelled to London so they could shop for the dress together and then had it delivered to Edinburgh, as she quite rightly said this would be much easier than Claire lugging it across the country.

Claire walked past the queues, having been able to check in electronically, and made her way to the nearest coffee shop. Her flight to Edinburgh wasn't flashing a boarding gate yet and so Claire figured she had time for a coffee and a quick bite to eat. Her carry-on suitcase, which she had checked matched the strict dimension requirements, was on wheels and she tugged it behind her as she joined the inevitable queue to be seated.

'Table for two?' the rather harassed looking waiter asked.

Claire tried to hide a sigh, feeling like it had begun already. Even the waiter was having a dig at her single status. It was probably just her imagination and she was a little over anxious. Claire knew that it would be a hot topic of conversation. She also knew that most of her friends were just trying to be kind and supportive but going on about it, asking her if she was lonely and trying to set her up with a series of unsuitable men, was not, in any way, helpful.

'Miss?' the waiter asked and he managed to sound both bored and impatient.

'Just one,' Claire said and tried to sound like that fact didn't bother her.

'We don't have any tables available,' the waiter said and seemed to be already moving on down the queue.

'Hang on!' Claire said indignantly. From where she was standing there were plenty of tables free. 'And what are those?' She pointed towards some booths that were unoccupied.

'They are for groups,' the waiter said as he stepped away from her.

Claire could feel the anxiety over meeting up with her friends who were, no doubt, going to question her on her love life, move to full-blown anger. Seriously, there were lots of things that single people had to put up with, and some of those things were thanks to a world that viewed people who weren't in couples as somehow second-class citizens but Claire had had enough.

'Are you discriminating against me?' Claire asked, glaring at the waiter, who didn't look particularly intimidated but at least she had his full attention again.

'Look, miss, don't have a go at me. I'm just following my boss's orders. I can't give a table for four away to a single person.'

'So what you are telling me,' Claire said, both hands on her hips and one single eyebrow raised, a technique she had perfected over five years of teaching, 'is that your boss is discriminating against me?' She didn't raise her voice — she didn't need to. Teaching had taught her that losing your temper didn't achieve the desired result.

The waiter looked somewhat like a trapped animal. It seemed clear that whatever his boss's instructions were, they hadn't covered what to do when faced with someone who questioned them.

'I'll get him for you,' the waiter said and scurried away.

Claire could feel the people in the

queue behind her shuffle their feet. She could pick out those that were English, since they were looking anywhere but at her and appeared to be embarrassed that she had challenged what was obviously a rule. Others, who were clearly not English, were making not so quiet comments about having to wait to be seated and how other people were preventing them from drinking their first coffee of the day.

The waiter returned, with an equally harassed-looking young man, who looked like he must have just left school. He was holding his hands out in front of him as if he was expecting to be physically attacked. Claire rolled her eyes. It wasn't as if she had even raised her voice.

'Are you the manager?' she asked, going for what she hoped would be interpreted as a light tone with absolutely no threat involved.

'The shift manager,' the young man said, although to Claire's ears he didn't sound completely sure and she felt a little guilty, even though she knew she had done nothing wrong.

'Well, I'm a customer and I would like to sit down. So perhaps you could show me to a seat.'

'I'm afraid we don't have any tables available,' the shift manager told his shoes, since that was where his attention was focused.

'Now that's not really true, is it?' Claire asked in her best teacher voice.

'I can't sit you at a table for four, it wouldn't be fair to the other customers,' the man said, once again to his feet, although this time at least he did manage to glance up in her direction.

Judging by the increased murmuring and feet shuffling, those same customers were getting fed up too and Claire suspected that she would be to blame, rather than the ridiculous policy of this particularly coffee shop chain.

'All I want is to sit down, order a coffee and maybe some food. So why don't you let me sit down and then the rest of these customers, who have been very patient, can also sit down and order.' Again Claire used her best teacher voice.

'I can't sit you at a table for four . . . ' He tried again and Claire imagined that whoever his manager was, had not covered what to do in this situation any more than he had with the waiter.

'How about if we share a table?' A voice sounded from further down the queue and Claire, the waiter and the shift manager all turned their heads in the direction of the voice. A tall man, wearing a black leather jacket and what looked to Claire to be motorbike boots, held up a hand. His voice had the tinge of an accent but Claire was unable to pin down where he might be from.

'Thank you,' Claire said, directing a polite smile in the man's direction, 'but I would like to drink my coffee alone and besides there is a principle at stake here.'

'I understand,' the man in the leather jacket said, 'but there's also a queue and a lot of people who look about ready for their morning cup of Joe and maybe some pancakes.'

Now Claire knew for sure that the man was American. She couldn't see an English guy making a scene like this.

'Am I right, people?' Leather Jacket said to the surrounding crowd, who all nodded and murmured and shuffled their feet some more.

'Now I appreciate there is a principle at stake but perhaps we could put that aside for now and go for a compromise instead?'

Claire looked from Leather Jacket to the waiter, to the shift manager and back to the queue and she knew that she had lost. If she were to continue to complain now, she would be the one making a scene.

'Well, I can't say I'm happy . . . ' Claire started to say.

'I'm sure that we can do something about that, can't we? A free coffee for the lady, or maybe a pastry, to make up for your rules?'

Leather Jacket was grinning broadly

and Claire knew it would be churlish if she didn't agree to at least share the table with the guy.

'We'll take that booth over by the window,' Leather Jacket said and headed off to the best seats in the house with the waiter trailing in his wake. The shift manager looked at Claire expectantly and so she trundled her carry on over to the table.

Claire pushed the handle back into the suitcase and then placed it on the booth seat, before scooting in beside it.

Leather Jacket was lounging back in his seat and ordering, it seemed, for both of them. The waiter scurried away as soon as he took the order, obviously worried that Claire was going to start again.

This gave Claire the opportunity to study the man, who seemed to believe he had come to her rescue like a knight in shining armour. Her first look made her cheeks colour. He was undoubtedly handsome and he had an easy smile. He seemed totally at ease with himself but

Claire wasn't sure if that was arrogance or confidence.

'Gabriel McKenna,' Leather jacket said with a broadening grin. 'Most people call me Gabe, apart from my grandma. With her it's always Gabriel whether I'm in trouble or not.'

'Claire,' she replied, not sure that she wanted to tell a complete stranger any more about herself, however charming he might appear.

Gabe nodded.

'Well, pleased to meet you, Claire. And what brings you to the airport today?' Gabe swung both arms along the line of the booth back. He looked so relaxed and Claire felt the complete opposite.

In her head she could hear her friends telling her to start talking. She was, after all, sitting opposite a handsome man, who looked the right kind of age and who appeared to be charming. And they were about to have coffee, which was the perfect first date situation. But this wasn't someone that her friends had recommended as being a nice guy, he was some random person she had met at the airport and if she was honest, Claire knew that she just wasn't good at the whole 'making conversation' thing.

The waiter brought the coffee and pastries and then dashed away, leaving Claire feeling a little uncomfortable and Gabe apparently unperturbed. Gabe took a sip and then helped himself to a Belgian bun. He chewed it appreciatively and raised an eyebrow. Claire took this as a sign that she should speak.

'I'm flying to Edinburgh,' Claire said.

'Me too,' Gabe said, using a napkin to wipe icing from around his lips and smiling. 'Going to visit an old buddy of mine.'

'Me too,' Claire said, taking a sip of coffee. 'I mean, I'm visiting some friends from university.' She didn't know why but she didn't want to mention the fact that she was going to a wedding.

'Did they move away or did you?' Gabe asked.

'Me, I guess. My family are all down south and I wanted to head back that way.'

Gabe nodded and Claire had the feeling that he was really listening. She had been on some dates before where the guy had barely listened to a word she had said. Needless to say there had been no second date. Not that this was a date, of course. Gabe was just a nice guy who had helped her out. She had let her imagination run away with her before and it had not ended well.

'It's my first time in the UK,' Gabe said. 'My buddy's family moved back to Scotland when we were both twelve but we kept in contact and he came out and visited a bunch of times. I figured it was about time that I was the one to take the long trip.'

'You didn't want to fly straight to Edinburgh?' Claire asked.

'Well, I figured if I was going to come all this way I should see some of the sights so I booked in a couple of days here in London.'

'Good plan. There's lots to see,' Claire said. She loved life in the city and always found there was more to explore than she had first imagined.

'I did the big tourist draws but I get the feeling that the best bits are kept hidden by you Londoners. I think maybe to really see London you need a local to guide you.'

'That's true. I have friends who've lived in London all their lives and there are some great places they've taken me that I never would have found on my own.'

'Well, if I'm ever back in town, maybe you could show me around?' Gabe's eyes sparkled at the idea and Claire smiled back as her mind kicked in with images of her and Gabe taking in all of her favourite places.

'I'd like that. There's some great places to eat that are off the beaten track, and there are some small galleries that have some unusual pieces. I mean, if you like art . . . ' Claire stopped talking and could feel herself colour up. She had no idea if Gabe liked art and felt foolish somehow. It was so like her to get on to a subject and just talk.

'I have to confess that I don't know much about it but I'm a quick study.'

Claire felt a little more at ease and smiled, which he rewarded with a grin and a nod.

'It's not like I'm an expert. I mean I like what I like, if you know what I mean?'

'I do, and I like the sound of that.'

'I just feel that art should be about what you see, not what some expert says you should see.'

Gabe seemed to take a moment to think about that and nodded.

'I never really thought about it but I like that approach.'

There was a ping and then a voice came out of the loud speakers.

'Flight BA two, five, four, three for Edinburgh is now boarding at gate six.'

'Your flight?' Claire asked. Claire was

flying on a cheap airline but couldn't quite picture Gabe doing the same.

'Yeah, but they make you wait for ages at the gate and I'd rather stay here with you.'

'But you might miss your flight.' Claire couldn't imagine just sitting here if her flight had been called. She knew that if it was her flight she would have to get up and walk to the gate, however much she might be enjoying her coffee with Gabe. But seemingly he was unfazed.

'Nah, I can run pretty fast.' He grinned at her.

'You're braver than me,' Claire admitted.

'Now that I doubt very much,' Gabe said with his head to one side and Claire got the feeling he was assessing her.

There was another metallic ping and this time it was Claire's flight. As she stood up, Gabe did, too.

'I was wondering if I could have your number?' he asked and for the first time he sounded less sure of himself or perhaps he just wasn't sure how Claire would react.

'How about we swap e-mail addresses?' Claire said and Gabe nodded although Claire couldn't tell if he was disappointed or not.

'Sure, that'd work,' Gabe said as he pulled a pen from inside his jacket and scribbled something on a clean paper napkin. He handed the pen to Claire and she wrote her e-mail address on a napkin and handed it back to Gabe.

She wondered what her friends would make of all this and whether it would be enough to keep their romantic fairy godmother approach at bay.

Gabe and Claire swapped napkins. He placed his carefully in his inside jacket pocket, whilst Claire folded hers and dropped it into the outside pocket of her carry on.

Gabe dropped some notes on the table and waved away Claire's offer to pay her half before she remembered that supposedly her coffee and cake were free anyway.

They walked out of the restaurant together and Claire got the feeling that the waiter and shift manager weren't sorry to see her go. For her part, the experience had not turned out how she expected, either.

Devastating News

Gabe led the way through the crowds, looking as if he knew where he was going. Claire had to scurry to keep up, all the while trying to spot a sign that would take her to her own boarding gate. It would be beyond embarrassing if she blindly followed Gabe and ended up at the wrong gate.

'That's you,' Gabe said, coming to a halt so quickly that Claire nearly ran into him as she was scanning for signs of her gate.

'That's me,' she said with a smile, hoping that he hadn't noticed quite how close she was and trying to casually take a step backwards.

'It's a shame we aren't on the same flight,' Gabe said and he did sound sorry, which sent a little fizz of excitement through Claire. Although she wasn't sure how she would have felt if he was on her flight. Wouldn't that be awkward? They had only just met and Claire wasn't used to just bumping into a person and hitting it off.

For starters, she didn't have much time for going out and it wasn't like she was a big fan of clubbing or anything like that. This was exactly the sort of thing that happened in books and in the movies but it didn't usually happen to her, which she supposed was one of the reasons she was still single.

'Well, bye then, Claire. Maybe I'll see you around.'

Claire's mind raced as she tried to think of something to say. This isn't hard, she told herself, but her mind remained stubbornly blank. Claire could feel her face colour as she realised that she hadn't responded to his comment in the way that was expected. She winced at the thought of what Gabe might make of her silence.

The whole dating/new relationship thing was full of pitfalls and Claire wondered if it was one of the reasons why she had avoided any active search for the man of her dreams.

'Bye, Gabe. Sorry . . . I was thinking about the flight and whether my friend will actually be on time at the airport.'

Claire thought she detected a slight change in Gabe's cheerful, relaxed outlook. Was he disappointed in her reaction? Claire stared at her feet — anything to avoid that expression. Why was she so bad at this? The answer was obvious, of course — it wasn't like she had had much practice. A small part of her, the part that still had childhood fantasies of how falling in love worked, believed that none of that mattered when you met the One. That you were just automatically at ease with them and there were no embarrassing pauses or hesitation.

'See you around, Claire,' Gabe said, holding up a hand in a sort of salute and then he walked off and was quickly lost in the crowd.

★ ★ ★

Normally during a flight Claire would be busy planning her stay, wherever she was heading. Normally she would be poring over the latest guidebook and triple checking her plan to ensure that she could make the most of her limited time.

She did have a guidebook for Edinburgh and once the wedding was over she knew she would have a couple of days to explore. The problem was, she couldn't think about that. All she could think about was Gabe. It was like being fifteen all over again, when she had fallen deeply and painfully in love with her older brother's best friend who was about as unreachable as any movie star crush might be.

She was feeling the same mixture of excitement and hopelessness which she had felt back then. Was Gabe as much out of her reach as Billy had been? She wasn't sure — but Gabe had seemed a little interested in her, unless he was just being polite or maybe that was just how American guys were.

Claire groaned quietly as she battled to make her mind make sense. The older business man, in his sharp suit, flicked his eyes in her direction as if he wanted to make sure she was all right but didn't actually want to have to engage in conversation, which was a relief to Claire. She was sure that anything she tried to say out loud would make her sound like a crazy person.

What she needed was to talk to Lorna. Lorna would help her make sense of anything and maybe she could suggest just what Claire should do with the e-mail address on the napkin in the pocket of her carry on.

★ ★ ★

The flight was uneventful and Claire was quickly making her way through to arrivals where Lorna had promised she would be waiting for her. Claire had said that she could make her own way to Lorna's flat if she had lots of wedding preparations to be going on with, but Lorna had laughed and said that it had all been organised months ago and besides, she had a checklist as always and everything was under control.

The big double doors opened and Claire was hit by a wall of noise from the arrivals hall. People milled around, others were hugging in small groups and others stood still holding signs with names on whilst still more stood on their tiptoes to see if their loved one was on their way through the door.

Claire walked forward slowly, pulling her suitcase and scanning the assembled crowds. Lorna should either be standing there holding a sign as a sort of joke or be bouncing up and down in excitement but Claire could see no sign of her.

She moved off to the side so that she wasn't blocking the flow of people moving through the doors and waited. As the minutes ticked by, Claire started to worry. Lorna was never late for anything. Claire had even joked to Jack that he would need to be at the church extra early since even the tradition of the bride being late wouldn't be enough to keep Lorna from arriving early herself.

Claire was just reaching into her bag to grab her mobile when she could hear running feet and someone calling her name.

Claire looked in the direction of the voice and could see her best friend Lorna weaving in and out of the crowds, waving her hands in the air and looking somewhat dishevelled.

'What's wrong?' Claire said, taking in her friend's hair, which was in a sort of lopsided pony tail, with strands splayed out in all directions. But more worrying was her face which was streaming with tears.

Claire pulled her friend into her arms. She could feel Lorna shake as the sobs she had been holding back moved through her body. All Claire could do was hold her and rub her back and tell her that everything was going to be all right. Claire was aware of the curious looks they were getting from the crowds.

'Why don't we go find somewhere to sit down?'

Lorna nodded and Claire reached down for the handle of her carry on, and with one arm still round her friend's shoulder she guided her in the direction of a nearby set of chairs, which thankfully were empty. They sat down and Claire squeezed Lorna's hand.

'Whatever it is, I'm sure we can sort it out,' Claire said, hoping that was true. Maybe Lorna was just overwhelmed with the wedding planning. It was only a few days after the end of term and last time they had spoken they had both agreed that they were ready for a holiday. Lorna was shaking her head and then there were fresh tears.

'We can't,' Lorna said shakily. 'It's Jack.' Lorna's face seemed to crumple with saying the name of her husband-to-be out loud. Claire tried to swallow the sudden lump in her throat.

Lorna and Jack had met in the first week at university and they had been inseparable ever since. Jack had proposed four weeks later and Lorna had laughingly turned him down, saying they were far too young. It had taken three more proposals and over five years until Lorna finally said yes. Surely Jack couldn't have changed his mind? Claire had never been more convinced that two people were in love.

'What about Jack?' Claire said, although she was almost too scared to ask for fear of what the answer might be.

'He's not going to make it to the wedding,' Lorna said, each word punctuated by a sob.

Claire frowned.

'I don't understand . . .'

'He's on a business trip and he can't get back in time.' Lorna looked Claire directly in the eye. 'There's been a volcanic eruption and the ash means that planes can't fly. He wanted to cancel the trip before he left, said it could wait till he got back from our honeymoon, but I told him to go.' Lorna was nearly wailing now and she seemed to realise it when an older couple looked at her disapprovingly so she clamped a hand over her mouth.

'It's all my fault!' Lorna said, her hand still muffling her voice.

'Oh, Lorna. You didn't know there was going to be an eruption. No-one could have known.'

'What am I going to do? Everything is paid for. Everyone has arranged their travel and their hotel.'

'Well maybe we can delay things for a week?'

'That's Trish and Jeff's wedding,' Lorna said and a fresh wave of sobs started.

Claire knew that she needed to take control. One thing was for sure, they weren't going to sort anything out if they stayed at the airport.

'Let's go back to your flat and then we will come up with a plan.'

'You promise?' Lorna asked, sounding so like one of Claire's students that Claire couldn't help smiling. She had no idea what could be done but she knew she would do whatever she could to ensure her best friend could marry the love of her life.

A Waiting Game

Claire had sat Lorna down on the sofa and made them both a cup of tea. Rifling through the cupboards she had found a packet of biscuits and then she plonked herself down on the sofa next to Lorna. She had a sip of tea and felt immediately refreshed. She took a deep breath and tried to work out exactly how she was going to save her best friend's wedding.

'Right,' she said, trying to inject some confidence in to her voice, 'tell me everything that has happened.'

Lorna sniffed and then helped herself to a tissue from the box on her coffee table.

'Jack rang me last night. He's in Finland. There's been a volcanic eruption in Iceland and there's a flight ban for all of northern Europe.'

Claire nodded. She thought she had

heard something about it on the news the night before but it hadn't registered.

'Do you remember the last eruption?' Lorna asked, her voice going up a notch or two. 'No flights for weeks — weeks!' Her eyes went wide as she seemed to realise what that might mean. Claire reached out and squeezed Lorna's hand.

'Breathe, Lorna. It's going to be OK.'

'How?' Lorna wailed and Claire had the impression that they were in for another round of sobbing if she didn't step in.

'Tell me exactly what Jack said. Did he say that he wouldn't make it back in time?'

'No,' Lorna said shakily. 'He said there were no flights and then he got cut off. I've tried ringing back but the internet says the mobile phone masts are down.'

'Did you ring his hotel?'

'They said he'd checked out.'

Claire nodded, taking all this in.

'Lorna, from what I know of Jack, and I've known him as long as you have, I expect he is finding another way to get back home.' Claire glanced at her watch and did a quick calculation in her head. 'OK, so he has, let's say, seventy-six hours to get back here.'

Lorna sniffed and looked up.

'Do you think he might?'

Claire smiled.

'I think we should assume he's going to. Otherwise he's going to look pretty silly standing at the altar waiting for you, after he's travelled all those miles, whilst you sit on your sofa in your jogging bottoms crying.'

'But how?'

'He'll find a way. Flying might be the quickest way but there's lots of other ways to travel — sea, train, car. Lorna, Jack would even walk if he had to. You know he would.'

Claire watched the sadness melt away from her friend's face to be replaced by a look of such hopefulness, that Claire could only hope her prediction was right.

'But how will we know?' Lorna asked.

'I'm sure he will call as soon as he can and if he can't, well, we'll just work on the principle that he is coming until we are told otherwise.'

Claire helped herself to a biscuit. She hadn't eaten since the pastry with Gabe and she was getting hungry. Her mind conjured up an image of Gabe but she pushed it quickly aside. She needed to focus and she didn't think now was a good time to bring up her crush with her recently distraught friend.

'So, where's the 'to do' list?' Claire asked and was finally rewarded with a smile.

★ ★ ★

The night before the wedding Claire found Lorna in what had become her usual spot. Lorna had been out and bought a map of Europe and pinned it to the wall of the lounge in her flat.

With pins and some red cotton, she had been tracking Jack's progress as he tried to make it home. Jack had rung several times whenever he found himself near a landline, usually at a train station, and updated them.

Every time Lorna had put a pin in the map and when she had more than one had started to map out Jack's route with a length of cotton.

Jack was heading for Brussels and the train that would take him across the channel. Once in London he was booked on the first flight to Edinburgh which would give him just under an hour to get changed and to the church. Jack was going to make it, as long as nothing went wrong.

Claire didn't need to ask what Lorna was thinking about. It was written all over her face. Would luck be on their side and mean that Jack had smooth travel right up to the altar?

'Here,' Claire said, handing Lorna a glass of wine. 'Pizza will be here in twenty.'

'I'm not really that hungry,' Lorna said, taking the offered glass but continuing to stare at the map.

'You need to eat,' Claire said in her no-nonsense tone, which she usually used at work when the children were playing up. Lorna flashed her a smile.

'I'm not one of the kids in your class, you know,' Lorna said.

'In which case you'll eat your dinner with no complaints.' Claire folded her arms and they both laughed. 'Staring at the map won't make him get here any sooner,' she added, before slipping her arm through Lorna's and dragging her away to the sofa. 'And besides, this is your last night as a single woman. At the very least we should do something fun.'

'Isn't this the point where you are supposed to offer me marriage advice?' Lorna said as she curled her feet up underneath her.

Claire mirrored Lorna's position but at the other end of the sofa and snorted.

'Like I know anything about it.'

Claire knew that Lorna was looking at her closely and wondered if now was the time to bring up her airport meeting with Gabe.

'Spill the beans,' Lorna said.

'About what?' Claire asked, suddenly feeling like if she spoke about Gabe the whole dream might shatter and she would wake up, and it never happened.

'There's something different about you. I've known you for years and I can tell,' Lorna said, leaning forward as if getting a closer look at Claire might somehow tell her what the secret was. 'And we haven't even had time to discuss your love life.'

Claire took a sip of wine and looked thoughtful.

'Did you meet someone?' Lorna asked. Claire was just trying to figure out how to explain what had happened at the airport when Lorna jumped out of her seat.

'You've met someone!' Lorna was bouncing up and down in the way that

Claire had expected her to at the airport.

'Calm down, will you?' Claire said, flapping her hands at Lorna, who did a little celebratory dance and then sat back down.

'Tell me everything,' Lorna urged.

'There's not really much to say. I wanted to get a coffee at the airport but you know what they are like, with all their rules. Can you believe they had free tables but they wouldn't let me sit at one of them because I was by myself and the tables were for four? I mean seriously in this day and age . . .'

Lorna held up a hand and looked expectant. A classic teacher move that worked on grown-ups, too. Claire stopped speaking.

'Stick to the facts,' Lorna said. 'No waffling allowed.'

'I'm not waffling,' Claire said indignantly, 'I am giving you the context.'

'Not interested. Get on with the important stuff.'

The doorbell rang and saved Claire

from having to argue that it was important. Only once they had paid the delivery man and both eaten a slice of pizza did Claire get back to the hot topic.

'He's American and he kind of came to my rescue. Suggested that we share a table, even got the manager to give me my coffee and pastry for free.'

Lorna had raised an eyebrow and Claire knew that she was being given a warning to get on with it.

'He asked for my number but I thought that might be a bit risky so I gave him my e-mail instead.'

Lorna stared and said nothing. Claire waited, knowing that a full analysis was coming.

'Right, I would have given him my number but I get it. You want to play it coy.'

That wasn't exactly it but it sounded much more reasonable than the actual reason, which is that Claire thought it might be a bit forward, giving out her number to a guy she had just met.

'So what did he say in his e-mail?' Lorna leaned forward with a cheeky smile on her face.

'What e-mail?'

'Claire, please tell me you have checked your e-mail since you got here.'

'I don't know if you noticed but I have been kind of busy,' Claire said, picking up a slice of pizza and taking a bite, hoping it would delay her having to explain herself.

Now she thought about it, she really should have checked her inbox. The problem was that she had been a bit scared to. Scared that it might be empty and that he had only suggested swapping contact details because he was being polite. The minute she checked and realised this the dream would be over and she wanted to put that off as long as possible.

'Claire! That's the worst excuse ever! If he's e-mailed you and you haven't replied he probably thinks you aren't interested.' Lorna flopped back on the sofa and then turned to Claire suspiciously. 'You are interested, aren't you?'

'Yes. I don't know. I think so. I mean, I spent all of thirty minutes with him so I don't really know him.'

Lorna laughed and Claire looked confused.

'You should look at your reflection in the mirror when you talk about your mystery man. You are smitten. It's written all over your face.'

'I think I have a major crush,' Claire said and as the full impact of that statement hit her she covered her face with her hands. 'And I'm too scared to check my e-mails.'

Lorna shuffled up the sofa and flung an arm around Claire's shoulders.

'Don't worry. We'll check them together.'

Claire fished her phone out of her pocket and handed it to Lorna.

'You do it.'

Lorna took the phone and pressed the icon that would take her to Claire's e-mail account.

'Let's see. You've been selected as a prize winner for a free draw.'

Claire rolled her eyes.

'Your library books are due back next Tuesday.'

'Lorna, please . . . '

Lorna gave Claire a quick grin and then returned to scrolling through e-mails. When she clicked the phone off, Claire knew without being told. There were no e-mails.

'If he's American, maybe he needs to be on Wi-Fi otherwise it probably costs him a fortune. I'm sure he'll get in touch.'

Claire wished she could be so certain. Gabe didn't seem to be the kind of man who wouldn't send an e-mail if he wanted to. Could she really complain, though? It wasn't as if she had sent one to him. Maybe he was waiting to see if she would get in touch? After all, she was the one who had insisted on swapping e-mail addresses rather than phone numbers.

Lorna's landline rang, shrilly, and

Lorna bounded off the sofa, grabbing the handset before it could ring again.

'Hello?' She sounded breathless and excited and Claire wasn't surprised. Everyone Lorna knew had been told to avoid ringing the landline because Lorna wanted to be sure that if Jack did ring, she wouldn't be engaged.

Claire was glad of the distraction as it gave her a few minutes to think. Was it too late to email now? If Gabe lived in America then was she just chasing an impossible dream? What future could they have living on two different continents?

Maybe it was just better to let it go and be content with the short-lived dream? Long distance relationships were complicated and fraught with heartache. No, she needed to focus, to focus on Lorna and the wedding and to put all ideas of romance out of her head.

Out of a Dream

Lorna was pacing and Claire couldn't blame her. It was an hour until the wedding and there was still no news from Jack.

'Lorna. Sit down and get your hair done. Jack did say that he might not have time to ring you if he was travelling.' She reached for her friend's hand and gave it a squeeze. 'Or maybe he's just being traditional? You know, not seeing the bride before the wedding?'

'That's seeing, not talking, and I need to know if it's worth getting all dressed up. If it's not going to happen I'd rather just stop it here.'

'And then what? Have to rush to get ready in five minutes when he rings to tell you he's at the church waiting for you?' Claire fixed a smile on her face and tried to ignore the nerves bubbling in her tummy at the thought that Jack, despite his best efforts, might not make it in time.

Lorna took a deep breath and allowed Claire to lead her to the chair that had been set up in front of the hairdresser's mirror. She sat down and Claire smiled at Lorna's reflection in the mirror.

'You're right, Claire. We'll all get ready and then . . . ' Lorna didn't seem able to finish the sentence and Claire placed a hand on Lorna's shoulder and gave it a squeeze.

'I'm going to go and get my dress on so I can come and help you get into yours,' Claire said, giving Lorna one last smile before she left the room.

As Claire climbed into her lemon 1950s-style tea length bridesmaid dress, all she could think about was what they would do if Jack didn't arrive. Mentally she made a list. She already had all the phone numbers for the caterers and the venue for the reception and since there could be no refunds, the guests might as well go and eat the food that had been prepared.

Claire couldn't imagine that Lorna would be in the mood to party but the other guests might as well. Claire knew that Lorna and Jack had saved up for over two years to afford their perfect wedding and Lorna was worried they would have to wait another two years or have a simple ceremony and no reception. Claire shook her head. It didn't bear thinking about.

With no news from Jack or his best man, all they could do was carry on and hope. The wedding car arrived on time and was dressed with pale yellow ribbons tied to the door handles. The young bridesmaid and ring bearer had travelled with their parents to the church and so that left Lorna, her dad and Claire to travel in the wedding car.

Claire helped Lorna slide into her seat and tuck in the skirts of her beautiful dress. Lorna's dad climbed in beside her and squeezed her hand, whilst Claire climbed into the front next to the driver.

'Let's take it slow,' Claire said to the driver who nodded. She had already explained the situation before Lorna had come out to the car.

The driver did just as promised and they drove the pretty route, cross country to the church. The sun was shining and it was a perfect day for a wedding, Claire thought, crossing her fingers and her toes.

The church came into view and Claire could see people arriving, all dressed up and wearing smiles. There was no sign of Ben, Jack's best man, which was the agreed signal that meant they were ready to go.

'I'm going to get out and check how things are. Perhaps you could take one more turn around the village?'

The driver nodded his understanding and once Claire had climbed out of the car, he drove off slowly. Claire took a deep breath and turned towards the church. Keeping her eyes scanning for the arrival of fast cars with late grooms in she made her way up the steps, wishing that she had chosen more sensible shoes. Claire reached out a hand for the rail that wasn't there and started to feel herself fall.

Claire braced herself for hitting the ground and wondered if her dress was going to survive the experience but it didn't come. Instead she found herself scooped up, almost like being thrown in the air like a toddler with his daddy.

'Steady on there,' a voice said and Claire had to blink, sure that her eyes were deceiving her. It couldn't be! He couldn't be here, not here, not now. She had just decided that she must have hit her head, knocked herself out and she was stuck in some kind of unconscious dream, when she heard him laugh. And it all felt very real.

'Well, I didn't think I'd be seeing you again, not so soon,' Gabe said and he looked both surprised and pleased, an expression that sent Claire's heart into overdrive and she was sure that Gabe would be able to hear it racing.

'Gabe!' She gasped. It was about all she could think to say.

'Who'd have thought it?' Gabe said and he didn't seem to be in a hurry to put her down and if Claire was honest she wasn't in a rush to find her own feet, either.

'Are you a friend of Lorna and Jack?' she asked, struggling to find something sensible to ask when she felt all of a flutter.

'Nope, never met them, but I'm staying with my best pal Henry for the summer and he's invited so apparently he asked if I could come along with him and Jen.'

Claire blinked again.

'Henry Tenant?'

'The very same. Do you know him?'

'I went to university with him,' Claire said. She was still trying to make sense of everything when she heard a car engine.

Peeking over Gabe's shoulder, she saw the wedding car pull up in front of the church lychgate and she was suddenly back on planet Earth. With reluctance she wriggled out of Gabe's arms and he supported her back to her feet.

'Do you know if the groom is here yet?' Claire asked, all the positive feelings of seeing Gabe again disappearing under the weight of the thought of having to tell Lorna that Jack was not here.

'Well I don't know what he looks like but I haven't seen anyone dressed the part.'

Claire looked stricken.

'Hey, I'm sure he'll turn up soon enough.'

Claire glanced at her grandmother's watch that she was wearing.

'The question is whether he will be here in time to get married.'

Gabe followed Claire's eyes as she looked to the door of the church and the vicar in full regalia. Claire knew that there was a second wedding booked for later that afternoon. The vicar had been very understanding and promised to hold off for as long as possible but if Jack was too late they would have to make way for the next wedding party.

'You're friends with the bride?'

'Best friends,' Claire said, looking back to the wedding car and wondering if she should tell the driver to take another turn around the village. She couldn't imagine how Lorna must be feeling and it made her sad for her friend. This wasn't how her wedding was supposed to be.

Claire was shocked when she felt the tears build. The last thing she wanted to do was cry and not just because it would ruin her makeup but more that Lorna needed her to be strong right now.

'I might be wrong but I think I may have spotted him,' Gabe said suddenly, throwing his arm around Claire's shoulders and spinning her around so that she was facing in the opposite direction. A black taxi cab screeched to a halt and two men jumped out. One of them, who Claire could see was Jack, was running and trying to tie his bow tie as he went.

'You go get your friend and I'll give you a wave when the groom is ready,' Gabe said, turning Claire back around and pushing her towards the path that would take her down to the lychgate and out to the road where Lorna and her dad were sitting in the car.

Claire walked as fast as she dared in her shoes and pulled the car door open. Lorna's face was a mixture of hope and fear.

'He's here, Lorn. He made it!' Claire said and her voice shook as she got the words out.

Lorna made a noise which was a cross between a squeal and a sob and held out her hand. Claire took it and helped her out of the car as Lorna's dad came to join them. Claire turned and looked to the church and Gabe was there with one hand in the air. He waved and gave them a thumbs up.

'Who's that?' Lorna asked curiously.

'You wouldn't believe me if I told

you,' Claire said, busying herself straightening out the skirts of Lorna's dress. When she had the skirts splayed out to perfection, Claire stood up and smoothed down her own skirts. Lorna was looking at her curiously and Claire sighed. It seemed that no-one was getting married until Claire spilled the beans.

'It's Gabe,' Claire said and could feel her cheeks colouring.

'You e-mailed him?' Lorna asked her eyes wide.

'No, apparently he is Henry's friend from the States.'

A penny seemed to drop for Lorna as she nodded.

'I had no idea,' she said.

'Me, neither,' Claire said and gave a shrug. 'But we can obsess about that later. I think your groom is waiting for you and since he has gone to so much trouble to be here on time, I think we should join him, don't you?'

Lorna nodded and took a deep breath. Her dad held out his arm and

she took it and together they walked up
the path, with Claire following in their
wake.

Heading for Heartache?

As Claire walked up the aisle, doing the usual step, step together and step, behind Lorna and her dad, she could feel herself shake. She should be relieved, after all, that at the last minute it had all come together.

She could see Jack standing at the front of the church, all dressed up in his morning suit — and his best man had even managed to sort out his tie — looking so happy that his face seemed to shine.

Jack's attention was focused on Lorna as she walked towards him. Claire was relieved but she also felt incredibly nervous. She made sure her smile was in place. This day was all about Lorna and Jack and the fact that Gabe had appeared out of nowhere should not distract her from her role as maid of honour.

As she moved closer to the altar, she kept her eyes fixed on the front, despite that fact that she desperately wanted to scan the congregation, on the bride's side, for any sign of Gabe. She knew that he was there, she could feel it, but she needed to focus.

When she reached the front of the church, she rearranged Lorna's skirts so that they fanned out beautifully. She stood to one side as Lorna's dad kissed her softly on the cheek and then took Lorna's bouquet.

Once the vicar started to speak, Claire forgot about Gabe, lost in the wonder of the moment that Lorna and Jack promised themselves to each other, for ever.

The best thing about weddings was seeing two people so in love commit to each other but, as a single person, the worst thing about weddings was seeing two people so in love commit to each other when you had no-one in your life who felt that way about you.

Claire clapped with the rest of the

congregation as Jack and Lorna kissed for the first time as man and wife. They seemed lost in the moment, as if they hadn't seen each other in years. Claire knew that it must have seemed that way for both Lorna and Jack, when they had been separated by an act of nature that could not have been predicted.

Jack and Lorna held hands as they walked down the aisle as music played and Claire fell into step behind them. Now it was impossible not to scan the guests for a sign of Gabe. She saw Henry first and he waved and Claire gave a little wave back before she was distracted by the sight of Gabe, standing next to him, his gaze locked on her as she walked past.

Claire hadn't really taken in what Gabe was wearing but now she could see he was wearing a navy suit with an open white shirt and a white carnation in his lapel. His sunglasses were propped on the top of his head and Claire could feel his blue eyes follow her down the aisle. She wanted to stop but she knew she couldn't. No, there would be time for catching up later.

The photographer took nearly two hours to take all the photos and even though Claire wasn't in all of them, Lorna had asked her to stay close by to help with her dress and her bouquet.

Claire tried to focus but it was difficult. All she could think about was Gabe. It seemed impossible odds to her — that she should run into him at a busy London airport and that he would then later appear at her best friend's wedding.

Claire was torn — was it fate? Had fate ensured they met again because they were meant to be together? In which case fate was pretty mean since after the summer, Claire assumed, Gabe would be going back to America. Or was it just some strange coincidence that didn't mean anything?

Maybe it could be just a summer romance? The problem was Claire knew that she wasn't that kind of girl. She couldn't give away her heart, not for six weeks. She knew it would be broken when the summer ended.

Claire's friends were quick to point out that one of the reasons she was still alone was that she had her heart set on the fairy-tale romance idea. Claire thought they were probably right but she couldn't change who she was and when she fell in love, she wanted it to be real and for ever. Otherwise she couldn't see the point when all that was at the end was heartache.

'You going to stand there daydreaming or are you going to go and get your picture taken?'

Claire jumped. It felt as if Gabe had materialised out of thin air and she could feel her cheeks colouring. She knew he couldn't read her mind but could he read her expression? Did he know what she had been thinking about?

Claire, of course, had no idea whether Gabe had any feelings for her at all. They had only just met and knew nothing about each other. As usual she was letting her imagination carry her away and Claire knew that had never ended well before.

'Claire?'

'Sorry?' Claire said, realising that she hadn't actually answered Gabe's question and not only that, she felt like everyone else was staring at her.

'The photographer's waiting,' Gabe said and he was smiling, in a kind of cheeky, mischievous way, which made Claire feel even more sure that he could read her mind.

'Right,' Claire said, feeling as if a spotlight had been turned on her. She hurried across the grass and stood in the gap that had been left for her. Lorna looked as though she was trying not to laugh and so Claire glared at her as she handed over the bouquet, before rearranging her own face to smile at the camera.

As the wedding photographer called time on the last snap, it felt like the guests could finally relax. As the party made its way to the wedding cars,

Lorna managed to catch Claire's arm.

'He is gorgeous!' she said as Claire made shushing sounds, sure that they would be overheard.

'Who is?' Jack said, leaning in to give Claire a hug. 'Thanks for keeping everything together, Claire, You're a star.'

'You two were getting married if it was the last thing I did,' Claire said, giving Jack a peck on the cheek and a smile, hoping that would be enough to get Jack off topic, especially since she had caught sight of Henry moving in their direction and Claire was sure that Gabe couldn't be far behind.

'So, who's gorgeous?' Jack said and his eyes sparkled as he saw Claire colour once more.

'Lorna, of course,' Claire said, a little too loudly to convince anyone, as Henry appeared beside them.

'You look stunning,' Henry said, leaning in to kiss Lorna on the cheek. 'You remember you said I could bring a plus one?'

'Jen, your soon-to-be wife?' Lorna said, raising an eyebrow at Claire.

'No, Jen was coming anyway,' Henry said, looking confused, and Claire almost felt as sorry for him as she did for herself.

'I know, I'm only joking,' Lorna said. 'You mean your friend from America?' Lorna stood on tiptoe and looked over Henry's shoulder in a show of trying to spot him.

'Gabe!' Henry shouted and Claire froze, knowing that Gabe was behind her, somehow. 'Come and meet the happy couple.'

Gabe appeared at Claire's side, all smiles and he shook hands with Jack and Lorna.

'And this lovely lady is Claire, a friend from uni and best friend of the bride, not to mention being a beautiful maid of honour.'

Gabe turned to Claire and held out his hand. Claire went to shake it but Gabe lifted her hand to his lips and kissed it.

'The lovely Claire and I have already met,' Gabe said, giving Claire the full benefit of his smile.

It was hard for Claire to drag her eyes away from Gabe but she did. She could see a penny drop for Jack and Henry just looked confused.

'Wait . . . ' Henry said. 'Claire was the girl at the airport?' He looked stunned, as if he couldn't work out the chances of that happening either.

'She sure was,' Gabe said.

Claire could feel excitement fizz up inside her. If Gabe had told Henry about meeting her, maybe that meant he had felt something, too? Maybe he wanted to spend some more time with her? To see what might be.

Something Stupid

'I should have guessed,' Henry said with a chuckle, 'when you described the scene. Only our Claire would take a stand against the tyranny of chain restaurants and their treatment of single women.' Henry's smile dropped a little when there was a slightly awkward silence.

Claire tried to keep the smile on her face but it was hard, since she felt a burning shame build up inside of her. To be fair to Henry that was exactly what had happened but the way that he had described it made her sound like a crusading man hater.

Even worse than that, her mind could picture Henry and Gabe having a good laugh over it. Claire knew that Lorna was looking at her and also knew that Lorna would know exactly how she was feeling, even if she was managing to hide it from the rest of the world.

'It's good for Claire to stand up for herself, don't you think?' Lorna said, her tone mild but her implication clear.

'Of course,' Henry said, locking on to the get out of jail free card that had been offered him, just as Jen gave him a dark look.

'One of the things I have always admired about our Claire,' Henry said, throwing his arm around Claire's shoulder and giving her a peck on the cheek. 'Sorry, foot in mouth as usual. You know I adore you,' he whispered so that only Claire could hear. Now Claire did manage a smile. Henry had been a good friend to her and if occasionally he spoke before he thought, then she wasn't going to hold that against him. She squeezed him back to let him know that he was forgiven.

There was a soft toot of the horn, which saved anyone else from having to start a new conversation and they all turned to see the white 1950s Bentley pull up outside the church lychgate.

'Well, Mrs Campbell, I think our carriage awaits,' Jack said, smiling down at his bride. Their eyes locked and their love was clear for all to see. Jack leaned down and kissed her softly on the lips.

'I think you might be right, Mr Campbell,' Lorna said and smiled up at her husband. 'Claire, your car should be here soon,' Lorna added and everybody laughed. 'What?' Lorna asked.

'We all know that you like to be in charge,' Claire said with a warm smile for her best friend, 'but this is your wedding day. Perhaps you could relax and enjoy it and leave everything else to me?'

For a brief moment, Lorna looked slightly horrified at the idea of losing her grip on her usual organiser role but when Jack gave her a squeeze she laughed.

'OK, but only this once and only because it's you,' Lorna said and gave Claire a quick hug.

'Good,' Claire said. 'Now if you would kindly wait here I will line up the guests and make sure they have followed the instructions on their wedding invitations and have brought only eco-friendly confetti.'

Claire bobbed her head and then moved away, speaking to the groups of people and asking them to line up on each side of the church path. Once the photographer was in position, Claire went back to Lorna and Jack and asked them to make their way to the car, which they did in a shower of bio-degradable coloured petals.

Claire waved as the pair drove off to spend a few precious moments alone before the reception began.

* * *

The delicious meal had been eaten, the toasts raised and now Lorna and Jack took the floor for their first dance and were soon joined by other couples. Claire stayed in her seat at the main table and was content to watch.

Jack's best man had only recently

been married himself and so Claire had declined his traditional offer of a dance and suggested that he dance with his new bride instead. She kept her eyes focused on the dance floor and tried to arrange her face into a 'content to sit and watch' expression which she hoped would negate the sympathy dance offers which she knew would be coming her way. Not easy when you were sitting at the top table all by yourself.

Once the dance was over, she knew it would be safe to go and mingle and to catch up with old friends, but it seemed churlish to interrupt the most romantic dance of the evening, particularly when all her friends were in couples and most were due to get married soon.

She watched Henry whirl Jen expertly around the room, laughing and smiling, as if there were a light behind her eyes.

It was surprising to Claire that she had no doubts about any of her friends' relationships. It hadn't always been that way. Henry's girlfriend before Jen had been a colourful character, with a penchant for gossip and game playing. Claire had not been keen, but Henry had appeared smitten, at least for a while.

Jen was perfect for Henry and Claire was glad they had found each other. She tried not to give way to the thought that immediately followed, in these types of situation, as she wondered if she would ever find her own soul mate.

'They make a cute couple,' a voice said in Claire's ear, making her jump. The owner of the voice was standing close by, which was necessary due to the loudness of the music.

'They do,' Claire agreed as Gabe pulled out the chair beside her.

'May I?' he asked and Claire nodded, just as Lorna whirled close by and gave her a wink, before turning her attention back to Jack. As Jack moved Lorna away, he gave Claire a quick thumbs up and Claire rolled her eyes. The top table was way too public for her liking but she couldn't think of a reason to move away from it.

'Henry's not always had the best taste in women,' Gabe said conversationally, 'but I guess you would know that more than me.'

Claire smiled.

'His first girlfriend at university comes to mind.'

'Ah yes, the awful Annabel,' Gabe said, grinning at her. 'Henry actually brought her over to the States and I didn't know what to say to him. He seemed to have fallen for her completely but I couldn't stand her.'

'Me neither,' Claire said, feeling herself start to relax a little. 'She was really good at playing his friends off against each other.'

'Yeah, I know. That's why I felt I needed to tell it like it was,' Gabe said, a little seriously now.

'It was you!' Claire said, louder than she meant. Gabe tried to look innocent but his grin broke through.

'We broke up for the summer,' Claire

continued, 'convinced he was going to marry her and then by autumn term he was back, but no Annabel. Henry never told us what happened.'

'Well, you know what it's like with your first love. Henry couldn't quite get over that someone liked him enough to date him and that seemed to have clouded his judgement.' Gabe leaned in conspiratorially. 'My buddy would never admit it, but deep down I think he was a little scared of her.'

Now they both laughed. Claire didn't blame Henry. They had all been a little nervous of the infamous Annabel.

'So how did you get him to end it?'

'Oh, I just told him a little story about what his future would be like if he didn't.'

'I'm guessing he was more scared of that than facing the wrath of Annabel?' Claire asked.

'I guess so. He went straight back to their room and told her that it was over.'

Claire winced. Even though she

hadn't much liked Annabel she could still feel for the girl and the pain that sudden announcement must have brought.

'Hey, don't feel sorry for her,' Gabe said, taking in Claire's expression. 'It turned out that she had her eye on a friend of a friend of mine and went off with him.'

Claire shook her head. She wasn't surprised. Annabel was the sort of person who had a backup plan.

'He works in IT, is ten years older than her and filthy rich. She's in her element. Or so I hear.'

'Who'd have thought Annabel would have got her happy ending,' Claire said and then blushed when she realised she had said it out loud. Gabe was looking at her thoughtfully and so she looked away, pretending to study the dancing, which had moved from elegant ball-room to 90s dance.

'Still waiting for your happy ending, huh?' Gabe asked and Claire felt the sting of the words, even though she knew they were meant that way. Americans are straight talkers, she reminded herself. You're just not used to men speaking so directly.

'Actually, I'm happy as I am,' Claire said. In her head it had sounded light-hearted and jovial but it came out rather pointed and Gabe looked a little taken aback. He leaned away from her slightly and nodded.

'Well, in that case I won't ask you to dance,' he said and stood up a little abruptly. He stood still as if he wanted to say more. 'I'm glad you're happy, Claire,' he said, studying her face, before quickly walking away.

Claire watched him go, until he disappeared into the crowds. It had been going so well and then her reaction to one comment had seemed to knock the conversation off its path. It had all been so relaxed and friendly and then she had said the wrong thing.

Claire shook her head as she wondered, once more, why she was so bad at this. Why had she felt the need to be so defensive? It wasn't as if Gabe was having a dig. He was just asking a simple question and yet she had reacted as if he had insulted her life choices.

Claire pushed her chair back. She would march to his table and talk to him. Explain that she hadn't meant it as it had come out and ask him to dance. She had never been keen on making the first moves like this, but needs must and all that.

She smoothed down her skirts and lifted a hand to check her hair was more or less in place and then walked down the three steps to the dance floor. Carefully she edged her way around the enthusiastic dancers and towards the ring of tables, that had been pushed back to make way for the dance floor.

She spotted Henry and Jen first. Henry had his arm around Jen and they were whispering together. Claire couldn't see Gabe but she wondered if he had made himself scarce to give them some privacy. She kept moving past, not wanting to interrupt but could see no sign of Gabe on any of the other tables and he wasn't at the bar. Then reluctantly she turned her attention to the dance floor.

She didn't want to see him there but there he was, dancing and smiling and looking like he was having the time of his life, with another woman, who seemed to be enjoying the dance as much as he was. And it was clear to Claire that Gabe hadn't given her another thought.

More Than Friends?

Claire had had to work hard to keep her feelings from showing. Thankfully neither Jack nor Lorna had spotted Gabe with his new woman and so Claire had been able to pretend that everything was fine.

It was also fortunate that Claire, as maid of honour, was in charge of arranging the going away party. With the fireworks prepped and the guests informed, Claire had helped Lorna out of her wedding dress and into her going away outfit. Lorna had chatted happily about how wonderful the day had been. It had been a magical day for Lorna and Jack and to Claire's mind that was all that had mattered.

Standing at the front of the hall, with her bouquet in hand, Lorna had turned away from the crowd of women and was preparing to throw. Although it was the last thing Claire wanted to do, she knew it would draw more attention if she didn't, and so, when urged, she stepped to the front of the crowd and held her arms up in the air, just as the other women and girls were doing.

The only difference between Claire and the crowd was that she was desperately hoping not to catch the bouquet.

As Lorna's arm went up in the air, Claire had a sense of impending doom. She tried to step sideways to allow someone else, anyone else, to catch the bouquet, but short of deliberately dropping it, there was no way out and the beautifully hand-tied creation fell neatly into her reluctant arms. There were murmurs of disappointment from the crowd of women and girls and cheers from the rest of the guests. Lorna sought her out and pulled her into a tight hug.

'I think you might have found The One,' she whispered excitedly into Claire's ear before turning her around so that Claire was face to face with Gabe. Lorna gave her a little nudge in the right direction, before grabbing Jack's hand and making her way to the exit.

Claire stared at Gabe as he smiled at her as if nothing had happened. Claire felt both confused and a little embarrassed. What right did he have to smile at her like that? When he had deserted her on the top table acting hurt at his perceived rejection and then not two minutes later she had found him dancing with another woman, as if he had no cares in the world.

'I have to go and make sure the fireworks are ready,' Claire said, hurrying past him and wondering what she was supposed to do with Lorna's flowers.

What she didn't see as she tried to quickly make her way through the crowd at the exit, some of whom seemed to feel the need to clap her on the back and congratulate her, not to mention those that were cheeky enough to ask who the lucky guy was, was the look on Gabe's face as she ran away.

Henry spotted it, though, and was reminded of the look on the prince's face when Cinderella left only her glass slipper behind at the stroke of midnight.

He looked down as Jen squeezed his hand. She, of course, was the reason he knew what the prince's face looked like, she being a massive fan of classic Disney as well as being the person in his life to make him understand what love looked and felt like.

'I know I've only just met Gabe but are you seeing what I'm seeing?' Jen whispered as she and Henry joined the end of the queue for the exit.

'I think so,' Henry said. One thing he knew for sure — he had never seen Gabe react like that. He'd had plenty of girlfriends but had always insisted on keeping it fun and light and gave the impression that he never wanted to be tied down. Could it be that Gabe was falling in love? Henry grinned at the thought, that and the fact that he couldn't think of a more perfect match for his American friend, than Claire.

Claire managed to keep the smile fixed on her face. She 'Oohed' and 'Ahhhed' at the fireworks and clapped as the bride and groom climbed into their well decorated car and waved enthusiastically as they drove off. But as soon as the car was out of sight, all Claire wanted to do was escape. Not that easy, since she had promised Lorna that she would make sure that everyone got taxis home or to their hotels.

As the clock ticked past one in the morning, Claire was exhausted and wanted nothing more than to fall into bed. Having checked with the hotel staff that all the guests were either on their way home or staying at the hotel, she decided that was her cue to make an exit. Not that she was going very far. Lorna had insisted on booking her a room at the hotel, since she would be the one doing most of the work on the wedding day and was no doubt in for a late night.

Late night? More like early morning, Claire thought. But she was grateful that all she had to do now was stagger up the large spiral staircase at the centre of the entrance hall to the hotel, which had once been a stately home. She pulled off her high heels, something she had been dying to do all night, and padded up the carpeted stairs.

The music had stopped some time before and since the bar had now closed, it was very quiet and Claire felt like she could have been walking up the stairs in the 1920s, where money and glamour were the privilege of the upper classes only. Mind you, she thought with a smile, she would probably have been a servant, if she had been born back then!

Claire was so lost in that thought that she hadn't noticed the other person on the stairs.

'Now that your duties are done, does

this mean you'll have some time for me?' Gabe said, as he stepped on to the stair above hers. Claire wobbled on the spot. She had no idea that anyone was actually still up, let alone waiting for her on the stairs. She reached out a hand for the bannister and steadied herself, not wanting Gabe to feel the need to step in and rescue her as he had done before.

She was so confused and didn't think that being held in his arms would provide her with any real clarification.

'Sorry?' Claire asked. She knew she was stalling for time but she felt she needed to, in order to work out exactly what was going on. Hadn't he walked off and left her, a few hours earlier? She seemed to have insulted him and then he had thrown himself into dancing with someone else and then after that he had been acting as if none of that had happened.

'I said,' Gabe said with a grin, 'that I was hoping to get a moment of your time, now that your maid of honour duties are over.'

Claire nodded slowly and tried to read some clue as to what Gabe was thinking from his face but all she could see was his smile and he was the man she had met in the coffee shop all over again.

The problem was, now she didn't know what to make of him. He had seemed so easy going, and admittedly she had reacted a little self defensively, but if he was going to storm off every time they didn't agree, then she couldn't imagine they had much of a future. She shook her head at the thought. That was what was the matter! She was getting way, way ahead of herself.

Gabe probably just wanted to be friends. He was over in the UK for six weeks and she couldn't imagine that he would enjoy being involved in the wedding preparations that must fill Henry and Jen's lives right now.

'Sorry. I have been a little distracted by it all,' Claire said and tried out a smile. If Gabe was only interested in being friends then none of the other stuff mattered. What was it to her, if he chose to dance with someone else?

'Jack and Lorna were lucky to have you,' Gabe said.

'It was all Lorna, she had a list for everything. I just followed her instructions,' Claire said with a shrug, even though she knew she was downplaying her role. With Jack being stranded abroad she had ended up doing much more than she had thought she would.

'I still think you were the only one to keep the ship on course.'

'Thank you,' Claire said, knowing that she was blushing at his compliments and not knowing what else to say.

'You are very English,' he said and at first Claire thought he might have been having a bit of a dig but in fact his eyes were dancing and this too seemed to be a compliment.

'I'm not sure I can take the credit for that,' Claire said, wondering where the conversation was going.

'Are you staying in Edinburgh? Or heading back home?' He pronounced it 'Ed-in-boh-row' which made Claire smile.

'What?' he asked and Claire giggled. 'I said it wrong again, didn't I? Jen keeps trying to fix my American but she's clearly not having any luck.' He ran a hand ruefully through his hair, and if anything it made him appear even more handsome.

'I am staying in Edinburgh,' Claire said when she had composed herself, 'at least for a few days. My next wedding is in York on Saturday.'

'Another wedding?' Gabe said, raising his eyebrows.

'Yep. I have one a week for the next five weeks.'

Gabe let out a bark of laughter but put his hand over his mouth when one of the receptionists gave him a stern look.

'You have a wedding every weekend? What are you? A professional bridesmaid?'

'Thankfully just an ordinary guest for the next one.'

Gabe still looked impressed.

'Well, I'm staying with Henry and Jen and they have a whole pile of wedding jobs to do on Monday so maybe we could meet up? Do some of the sights together.'

Claire paused. She really wasn't very good at reading people. Small children she had down pat but grown-ups, not so much.

Was Gabe just being friendly or was he hinting at something more? Her heart fluttered and she told it to behave. After all, what did it matter?

Centre of Attention

Claire had had a leisurely Sunday morning. Having fallen into bed just after one she allowed herself a lie-in and was surprised by breakfast in bed at nine, which Jack and Lorna had organised.

It felt supremely decadent to Claire to be lying in a four-poster bed with the curtains open, looking out over the hotel's expansive grounds, eating a full Scottish and sipping a bucks fizz but she was determined to enjoy it.

After breakfast and a soak in the claw-footed bath, Claire plugged in her phone, which had gone flat without her realising it and she was greeted with the familiar beep of messages arriving.

One was from Jack and Lorna, with a photo of them at the airport as they waited for their flight to Paris. They were effusive in their thanks and clearly totally overjoyed at finally being married. Claire couldn't help smiling, too. It was lovely to see two of her favourite people so happy.

It had been Claire that had suggested Paris as a honeymoon destination, having visited and fallen in love with the place on her previous year's summer holiday, travelling around Europe.

She typed a quick message and sent it off, thinking that they probably wouldn't receive it until after they arrived. The little message icon told her that she had an e-mail as well and she bit her lip. Her heart told her it was from Gabe. He had promised to e-mail to confirm their plans for Monday and she felt a quiver of excitement at the thought. But what if it was just a junk mail? It would be a shame to ruin a perfect morning with disappointment. Claire looked up and caught sight of herself in the mirror.

'You are being ridiculous,' she told her reflection. 'You're not a teenager. Stop imagining what life could be like if

Gabe suddenly decided that he loved you! After all, in six weeks he's going back to America and then what are you going to do? Become pen pals?'

Claire had to stop herself from wagging a finger and laughed. Honestly! It was one day out. A day when Henry and Jen were busy and Gabe clearly didn't want to sightsee on his own. Claire never minded, in fact she always felt more of an explorer on her own but that didn't mean she couldn't appreciate a little company. Particularly when that company happened to be extremely handsome, with a lovely accent, Claire's teenage self pointed out.

She giggled again at how ridiculous she was being and then forced herself to click on the icon that would take her to her email account. There were two e-mails, one from her bank telling her that her online statement was ready to be viewed and the other was from Gabe.

Claire skimmed the e-mail, for a

moment worrying that Gabe was going to claim to have other plans. But when she read his suggestion that they meet at the Waverley Bridge at 10 and find somewhere to have coffee, she couldn't help herself and started to bounce around the room, squealing with excitement.

Claire had moved from the posh stately home hotel to much more modest accommodation, a B and B run by a young Scottish couple. If she were honest, although the luxury at the hotel had been fabulous, she was much more at home with the en-suite shower and room that barely fitted a double bed and small wardrobe.

It was hard, she thought, to imagine yourself having an adventure if your room came complete with a personal butler and 24-hour room service. No, she was much more suited to staying where you had to leave your room by 10 and couldn't be back until six. At least then you had no real choice but to go out and see the world.

So, unlike the morning before, she was up and dressed and eating breakfast in the communal dining-room at eight-thirty. She had spent the day before studying various guide books to Edinburgh and had a tentative plan in her head as to what she and Gabe should try to fit into their one day together.

Part of her wondered if he would want to spend more time with her but she quickly quashed that idea. He was a guest of Henry and Jen's and Henry would certainly want to make the most of the time he had with his American friend. It would be selfish of her to even suggest it and besides that, she didn't know if Gabe would even want to spend more time with her.

No, disappointment lay that way. What she needed to do was relax and enjoy the day and think about all the adventures she could have on her own.

Claire was way too early to be waiting at the bridge. Whilst she knew she was fairly clueless about dating — not that this was a date, of course — she also knew enough to realise that turning up more than an hour before the intended meeting time was just plain sad.

So instead she decided to take herself on a little walking tour of the city, one that she had worked out would deliver her to the bridge at precisely nine fifty, which seemed to her a perfectly acceptable time.

At 10 o'clock, Claire felt like she had been waiting for hours but then she noticed Gabe strolling through the crowd, apparently oblivious to the effect he was having on everyone around him. When he caught sight of Claire he smiled and raised a hand in greeting.

Claire was now sure that the crowd was staring at her. She felt colour rise in her cheeks but for once she wasn't bothered. This was the kind of attention that no woman minded. A group of young women, maybe a couple of years younger than Claire stared open-mouthed as Gabe pulled Claire into a tight hug.

Claire allowed herself a moment to get lost in his arms but then couldn't risk a sneaky glance at the group of young women, who were now whispering and giggling.

'It's great to see you again, Claire,' Gabe said and Claire felt like they were seeing each other for the first time in years, rather than days.

'You, too. I'm glad you could make it.' All thoughts of her tour of Edinburgh plan were gone from her head. She knew that she would be happy to follow Gabe wherever he wanted to go.

Gabe released her and Claire was sure she detected a hint of regret in his actions, which made her heart fizz once more. He seemed to be undertaking a close study of her features and so Claire looked away, worried that if she looked into his eyes, she might say out loud all that she was feeling on the inside.

'Well, tour guide, where do we go first?'

'Anywhere you like,' Claire said

dreamily, before taking in his slightly amused expression. Claire looked at her feet and gave herself a swift but silent talking to.

'Where would you like to go?' she asked once she had reined in her emotions. 'I have a sort of plan in my head,' she added.

'Sounds great, but I do have one request.'

'OK,' Claire said, wondering if it was one of the things she had on her mental list.

'I'd like to go and get a kilt for my clan.'

Claire's mind raced with images of Gabe in a kilt and they were all good. It took her a couple of seconds to realise that she hadn't actually replied.

'Of course . . . ' she managed to say, although worried that her comment sounded overly enthusiastic, as Gabe had that same grin back on his face.

'I want a real one, not a tourist one,' Gabe added.

'I know just the place,' Claire said.

She had planned to taken them there anyway. The Royal Mile was a place to visit if you came to Edinburgh and besides there was an old family-run kilt makers there which she knew would be perfect.

Claire had to fight the urge to reach for Gabe's hand but the idea that she might have misread what her heart was considering 'signs' as more than they were intended, stopped her. Perhaps he was just a friendly American. It would be mortifying to make a move, even a harmless one like that, only to discover that he didn't feel the same way.

'We need to head this way.' Claire said instead, holding out her hand in the direction they needed to go, not unlike a tour guide, and together they walked off the bridge.

'I'm hoping I've got the knees to carry this off,' Gabe said and he was grinning again. Claire nodded. She couldn't agree more.

In His Kiss

Claire was sitting in the kilt shop gazing around at the vintage wooden furniture. There were rows of wooden and glass cabinets that showed off the shop's wares and shelves lined every available wall space. She felt like she had stepped back in time to a different era and it was fascinating. Everyone who worked at the shop wore kilts, and since they were different patterns and shades, she could only assume that they were wearing their own family tartan.

'Your family tartan is the Monaghan County Tartan,' an older man said to Gabe as he ran a tape measure around Gabe's waist, 'and a fine tartan it is, too.'

The older man held out a hand and Gabe followed him through a set of curtains to what was presumably the dressing area behind. A younger man hurried after him carrying a range of kilts. Claire only caught a flash of colour but she thought she had seen earthy green and orange with a hint of purple. It reminded her of the Highlands and she thought it would suit Gabe's colouring perfectly.

Idly she wondered if he would wear it at Henry's wedding, later in the summer. That was something she wouldn't mind seeing.

She was lost in her dream world and didn't realise that the older man had pulled back the curtain and that Gabe had re-entered the shop. Gabe was dressed in the full Highland with a white shirt, waistcoat and black brogues, not to mention his new kilt.

'What do you think?' Gabe said and Claire couldn't help but smile at his slightly nervous expression.

'You look like a true Scot,' Claire said and Gabe visibly relaxed a little.

'I was thinking I might wear it to Henry's wedding . . . What do you think?

Jen's family will all be in traditional dress.'

'If that is the case, sir,' the older man said with the hint of a bow, 'then there are some further items of dress you will need for such a formal occasion.'

Claire watched as the man produced a kilt jacket and slipped it on to Gabe's shoulders. Claire's eyes went wide. Gabe was handsome, there was no doubt about that, she had thought it the moment she first saw him, but to see him dressed for his clan was something else and she felt her heart leap at the sight of him looking in the mirror self-consciously.

'It's very fitting for the occasion, Gabe,' Claire said, trying not to stare and act relaxed — a mighty hard thing to do with Gabe looking so incredible.

Somehow his flash of self-doubt made him appear even more handsome. She saw him search for her face in the reflection in the mirror and their eyes locked. Claire smiled in what she hoped was an encouraging way, and not one that would give away her initial reaction to seeing him in a kilt. Gabe grinned back.

'You heard the lady,' he said to the older man. 'I'll take the lot.'

By six-thirty, Claire's feet were aching. They had walked non-stop, except for the bus tour they had taken of the city. She was used to being on her feet all day but this was something else. Gabe had been as enthusiastic as she was to see the sights and so they had kept going long after she probably would have retired back to her B and B room.

'I'm starving,' Gabe said as they climbed off the tour bus for the last time. 'Do you fancy grabbing something to eat?'

Claire bit back a smile as he was obviously making some effort to sound casual, as if it didn't matter to him one way or the other.

'Sure, that would be nice,' she said. After all, she had to eat and better to eat with company than all alone, she told herself. Deep down she knew that wasn't the reason she had said yes. In truth, she didn't want the day ever to end. Gabe was the perfect tourist companion, not to mention the fact that he was charming and interested and all around the perfect man — except for the fact that he lived on the other side of the world, of course.

Claire shook her head. Trust her to fall for someone, after years of being single, who was geographically unattainable. And that was before she wondered what he felt about her.

They found a small Italian, away from the main tourist areas, and ordered. Judging by the accents of the waiting staff, they were in for the real deal when it came to the food.

'So how did you manage to get so long off work?' Claire asked. Gabe had already mentioned the fact that in America most people only got two weeks' leave a year. Claire couldn't imagine coping with just that. By the time the summer arrived, it wasn't just the children who were in need of a break.

Gabe did a half shrug and looked a little uncomfortable and Claire felt wrong footed. What could be wrong with that question?

'I didn't mean to pry,' she hurriedly added. The last thing she wanted to do was break the mood that had been with them all day. Considering they had just met each other, the day had been relaxed and happy.

'No, it's fine,' he said, running a hand through his hair. 'I guess I've just been trying to avoid that one.'

Claire didn't know what to say to that. She felt even more intrigued but she wasn't going to push. She hated when people did that to her — usually about her single status and the obvious question as to whether she wanted to have children, a question that she thought was an incredibly personal one to ask.

To her relief, their drinks arrived and their conversation moved back on to safer ground, although she did make a mental note to ask Henry next time she saw him. Whatever Gabe didn't want to talk about couldn't be that bad, could it? Maybe he had lost his job and didn't want to say.

'Did you always want to be a teacher?' Gabe asked, taking a sip of his beer and nodding approvingly.

'Since I was small,' Claire said with a smile. 'I was one of the few children who seemed to want to be at school.'

Gabe laughed.

'And does it meet your expectations?'

Claire took a moment to consider this.

'It's really hard work and there is more bureaucracy than I ever imagined. But when I am actually teaching . . . that I love.'

'How old are your students?'

'Eight to nine.'

'That's a great age. I have two nieces and three nephews and they were such fun at that age.'

Claire nodded.

'I'm the youngest by quite a long way,' Gabe said.

'I'm an only child.'

'I felt kind of like that,' Gabe said. 'My sister is eleven years older than me and the others older still. So by the time I was at school they had all left home for college — except Mattie who was in her last year of high school and resented being the babysitter.'

Claire smiled. It was hard to picture Gabe that young.

'And I bet you didn't make it easy for her,' she said.

'Let's just say I was a trouble magnet,' Gabe said with a grin.

'I can only imagine.'

They ate and talked and before Claire knew it, the restaurant staff were starting to pack up for the night.

'We should probably be going,' Gabe said as one of the waiters brought in the sign from outside. Gabe pulled out some money from his wallet and left it on the table. Claire opened her mouth to point out that they had agreed to share the bill but Gabe waved her protest away before it started.

'I'll walk you home — unless you want to get a cab?'

The night was warm and the stars were out as Claire looked up at the sky.

'Walking would be lovely,' she said, thinking that it would also be romantic but tried to push the thought away. She was only going to see Gabe once more, at Henry and Jen's wedding, and then he would go home. As much as she liked him, she wanted to save herself from the heartache of falling in love, or at the very least stop herself falling too deeply. 'It's not far,' Claire added, 'and we can get you a taxi back to Henry and Jen's.'

Gabe nodded.

'I'm not sure that I know my way enough to risk walking,' he said with his now trademark grin.

The walk took less than ten minutes and Claire could only wish that it took longer. They stopped outside the steps up to the grey stone house that was her

B and B and it felt like neither of them wanted to be the first to say goodbye.

'Well, I guess I'll see you at Henry and Jen's wedding,' Claire finally said, knowing that however much she might want to stay where she was, she needed to go inside.

'I'll be there and kitted out for the part,' Gabe said but his grin looked a little sad.

'I've had a lovely day, thank you,' Claire said. Gabe looked like he was going to say something and she wasn't sure her resolve could stand up to it. Gabe's eyes were fixed on her face and Claire couldn't look away.

'The perfect day,' Gabe said softly and then leaned in to kiss her softly on the lips. Claire knew that she should step back and pull away but instead she found herself kissing back and it felt like time had stood still. When they finally stepped away from each other, Claire could see the emotions she was feeling reflected in Gabe's face.

'I should go,' Claire said once more,

even though her feet were refusing to respond to her commands.

'I should, too,' Gabe said but he didn't move either. 'Will you still be in Edinburgh on Thursday? I have to pick up my kilt and I thought we could meet up.'

Claire had been planning to get the train to York, where the next wedding was, on Thursday but it wasn't as if she had booked tickets or anything and she was sure the B and B would have room to let her stay another night.

'Sounds good,' she said and some of the tension seemed to leave Gabe's shoulders.

'Great. I'll text you and we can arrange a time.'

Claire nodded as her heart seemed to quicken at the idea of seeing Gabe again so soon.

'I'll see you Thursday,' Gabe said and this time he did manage to take a few steps away. He raised his arm in a wave.

'Wait! Don't you want to get a taxi?' Claire called after him.

'Nah, I think I'll walk,' he said, walking away.

'But you don't know the way,' Claire pointed out, feeling a pinch of worry. She didn't want Gabe wandering around all night.

'I'll figure it out,' Gabe said. 'See you soon, Claire.' And he kept walking. Claire watched until he was out of sight and then climbed the steps to her temporary home.

All she could think about was seeing Gabe again and although she knew she shouldn't, although she knew that she had heartbreak in store when he went home, she couldn't quite keep the silly grin off her face.

Perfect Plan

The days had seemed to drag for Claire, even though she had headed out of Edinburgh on day trips. They were all things that she had been looking forward to, that she had been planning since the start of the summer term but still, the days dragged.

Monday hadn't felt like that, with Gabe by her side. He was as enthusiastic as she was and great company — not to mention the fact that her heart had been trying to tell her that he was the One. All she could think about, wherever she went, was what Gabe would have thought, what he would have enjoyed and wish that he was there by her side.

But Gabe was with Henry and Jen and Claire would never keep Henry from precious time with his best friend, that wouldn't be fair. Gabe had been in regular contact via his mobile and so she knew exactly what they had been doing, what fun they had been having.

Each time her phone beeped she wondered if this time, Gabe would invite her along. But then she had told him about all her plans, so to be fair, he probably thought she was busy doing her own thing, which she was, just wishing that he was there with her.

Her mind kept asking the question as to whether he was missing her as much as she was missing him, to the point that she felt like she was torturing herself. Why else would he want to meet up with her again, unless he had, at the very least, enjoyed her company? And then there was the kiss. He had kissed her first and had seemed as reluctant as her to end the evening.

No, there was something between them, she was sure of it. And Gabe had given every indication that he felt that way, too. But none of that changed the fact that he would be heading home at the end of the summer. Heading back to America and she would head back to London, thousands of miles apart.

Now it was Wednesday night and Gabe had suggested they meet at the kilt shop at 11 and then go and find somewhere to have lunch. Claire had forced herself to wait at least 10 minutes before replying. She didn't want to give the impression that she had been checking her phone every 30 seconds since she woke up, even if that was exactly what she had been doing. Claire knew enough about romance to know that probably wasn't something she should share.

Her mind replayed Monday and once again she came back to the mysterious conversation about how he had managed to get six weeks off work. Claire had come up with no better explanation than the fact he didn't have a job but that didn't really explain his generosity or the money he had to spend. She was desperate to find out but didn't want to push either so could only hope that Gabe would tell her of his own accord.

Claire's phone pinged and she saw another message had come in from Gabe.

'Can't wait to see you tomorrow!'

Claire felt the now all too familiar thrill and her heart flutter. She knew she was getting way too excited, letting herself get far too carried away but she couldn't help herself. She felt like she had waited all her life for Gabe to appear and not even the fact that he lived on the other side of the world could dampen those feelings right now.

The only thing nagging at the back of her mind was the secret he seemed to be keeping. Why didn't he want to tell her why he could take six weeks off from work? What was he trying to hide? There was nothing for it, she needed to stop being so English and simply ask him.

Claire was awake early, which wasn't too much of a surprise. She used the time to pack up her things. She was going to have to take her suitcase with her as she would be travelling to York at some point after meeting Gabe. Thankfully, she was used to travelling light and so it was a small case on wheels. She took as much time over breakfast as she could and then headed out.

She needn't have worried as, even though she was early, Gabe was lounging on a bench near the kilt shop waiting for her. She smiled to herself, sure that there was something between them and that it hadn't all been in her fevered imagination.

'Claire! Hi! I'm glad you're early. Henry dropped me off on his way to work.'

Claire smiled but felt her confidence slip slightly. Of course he hadn't been as desperate to see her as she had him, he had simply needed to get a lift in. Real life was not like the movies, she told herself firmly, and as a friend had once said when Claire had been despairing that she would never meet the One. There were no perfect Prince Charmings, there were ordinary men whom you loved enough to overlook their inevitable flaws and vice versa.

'How are Henry and Jen doing?' Claire asked, realising that Gabe was studying her in the silence.

'They're fine. Jen is doing a lot of running around and giving Henry instructions.' He smiled. 'Henry doesn't seem to mind at all.'

'That sounds like Henry,' Claire said, relieved that the conversation had moved her mind on from her thoughts of romance. She knew she should just focus on enjoying her time with Gabe. It was clear this was just going to be a summer friendship. He would head back to America and she would go back to teaching but at least she would have some good memories to take with her.

'Since we're early, should we go grab a coffee?'

'Sounds good,' Claire said as Gabe stood up and relieved her of her suitcase. Claire was going to protest that she could manage but held her tongue. It was quite nice having a guy around to do gentlemanly things for her. Not that she wasn't capable of doing all those things herself — she had had to — but it was nice all the same.

They wandered through the streets of Edinburgh with no real direction in mind. They had passed several coffee shops but Gabe showed no sign that he wanted to stop and so Claire said nothing, happy to walk by his side and chat. Finally, when Claire thought they were going to walk beyond the city centre, Gabe stopped.

'How about we get takeout and go to the park?' Gabe said, indicating a green space which had benches. 'It's a lovely day, seems a shame to stay inside.'

'Lovely,' Claire said and they went in together and ordered before finding a bench with some shade and a view of the park.

'I'm glad you could delay leaving,' Gabe said. Claire sneaked a look at him and could see he was smiling.

'I didn't have specific plans in York and the rest of the gang won't arrive until Saturday.'

'I did wonder if Henry would be going,' Gabe said, obviously trying to sound casual but failing. Claire felt her heart respond to the comment.

'I think he and Jen were invited but he didn't think you would fancy going to a wedding every weekend whilst you were over here.'

'I wouldn't have minded,' Gabe replied, turning to face her and flashing her a smile that made her feel dizzy. Claire would definitely not have minded either and wondered if they could both still come but then remembered a conversation she had had with the bride about guest numbers and catering.

'Who'd have thought that you were a fan of the weddings of complete strangers?' Claire teased.

'It's not weddings that I'm a big fan of,' Gabe said, looking at her. His expression was more serious now and he almost looked nervous. Claire opened her mouth to say something but having no idea what to say, closed it again. Gabe was silent for a moment as if he was assessing what his next move should be.

He raised an eyebrow as if he was checking that Claire understood his message but Claire could not trust her own reading of the situation, she needed Gabe to say it out loud.

'Oh?' she managed to squeak.

'That would be you, Claire.'

Claire nodded dumbly, as if he had just said that he preferred chocolate ice-cream to strawberry. When she saw a flash of disappointment in his eyes she felt panic overwhelm her. She needed to say something, to tell him that she felt the same too.

'I'm a fan of yours, too,' she said, the words coming out in a jumble and she felt her ears burn in embarrassment as Gabe laughed. When he saw the horrified expression on her face, he leaned towards her and kissed her gently on the lips.

'I'm sorry I laughed,' he said a little breathlessly when they had broken apart, 'but you are so English.'

Claire smiled, all embarrassment gone.

'I'm afraid there's not much I can do about that.'

'I wouldn't want you to change a thing,' Gabe said, picking up Claire's hand in his own.

'So, I was thinking I might like to see the sights of York.' His grin turned cheeky. 'What do you think?'

Claire kept her expression straight.

'I'm told there are some incredible sights worth seeing.'

'The thing is, I'm an American tourist. I'm not sure I could find my way round by myself.'

'Here's the funny thing,' Claire said, not being able to hold back her smile. 'I'm heading there and it just so happens that I know my way round.'

Claire held Gabe's gaze until he leaned in to steal another kiss.

'Perfect,' he whispered, although whether he was talking about Claire, or their plans, Claire wasn't sure.

Strange Behaviour

Claire still couldn't believe what was happening. Gabe was sitting beside her on the train and was coming to York with her. She had dreamed of spending more time with him but had thought it was impossible. She turned to Gabe.

'Are you sure that Henry doesn't mind? I feel like I've kidnapped you,' Claire said, not for the first time.

'Relax, Claire. If anything, I think he and Jen are quite happy to have a weekend on their own. They're about to get married. I'm sure they can cope without a guest for three days.' Gabe picked up Claire's hand and squeezed it reassuringly. 'And besides, I think Henry was keen for me to spend more time with you.'

'Oh yes?' Claire said innocently.

'Hmm. I overheard him and Jen.

Apparently they think we are perfect for each other.'

Claire smiled but a small voice in her head reminded her of two things. One was the fact that Gabe lived on the other side of the world and the other was the secret that Gabe was keeping. It wasn't that she thought she should know everything about him right now, they had only just met for goodness sake, but it was the fact that she had asked him what she assumed was a straightforward question and he had avoided answering it. Would he be the sort of man who kept lots of secrets? Claire wasn't sure she could cope with that.

She pushed the thought from her mind. She only needed to worry about that if things got serious and that wasn't possible. She needed to relax and enjoy each day but that had always been her problem. She was a planner and liked to know where she was headed in life.

Perhaps that was why romance had always seem so out of reach? It wasn't something that was easy to plan and maybe that was why she had shied away from it, or even put potential romances off. Well, she wasn't going to do that this time. This was her summer break and she was going to make the most of all of it — and that included her summer fling.

'I have a surprise for you, actually,' Gabe said, cutting through her thoughts.

'Oh?'

'I know that you were booked into a bed and breakfast but I thought I would treat you to a few nights in a nice hotel.'

Claire knew that her face was giving away her thoughts but she couldn't seem to help it. Gabe just looked amused.

'Relax, Claire, I booked two rooms.'

Claire did relax but now felt embarrassed at her reaction.

'I'm sorry, it's just . . . ' She didn't know how to explain.

'I'm not that sort of man,' Gabe whispered and Claire could feel herself sigh and then smile, 'but I am hoping you will let me treat you, whilst we are here.'

Claire was normally a 'go Dutch' kind of person but it wasn't a terrible thought that someone wanted to treat her. That and the fact that she had a small budget for her summer adventure and knew it wouldn't stretch to hotel accommodation.

'That would be nice,' Claire said and watched as Gabe laughed again, no doubt at her 'Englishness'. She grinned back at him. 'I daresay I can cancel the B and B.'

'Well, tour guide, perhaps you would like to tell me about the sights of York that I can expect to see?'

When they arrived at York station, Gabe insisted on getting a taxi. Claire usually walked to her accommodation or got the bus but decided not to argue.

'The Principal Hotel, please,' Gabe said.

Claire was staring at Gabe. The Principal? That was the most luxurious hotel, not to mention the most expensive — not that Claire had ever been there but she had heard about it.

'You do realise it's just round the road, mate?' the taxi driver asked, looking at them both in the rear view mirror.

'Happy to pay whatever,' Gabe said. 'I want us to arrive in style.'

The taxi driver shrugged and pulled out on to the road. Claire stared out of the window as the driver quickly took a turning and the hotel itself came into view. One glance at the real thing and Claire knew that she didn't have the right outfit to go to breakfast, let alone dinner.

She had the dress she was going to wear to the wedding, but other than that all she had was casual, tourist clothes. But she didn't have time to think about it any further as a man in top hat and tails walked towards the taxi and opened the door on Claire's side.

Claire stepped out and Gabe walked around to her side. The taxi driver unloaded the luggage and a bell boy with a gold metal luggage trolley appeared.

Gabe and Claire walked through the main entrance and up to reception. It was an old mansion, and had clearly been the home of a once great family. Huge chandeliers hung from the ceiling and a wide staircase was the main feature of the reception area. Portraits through the ages adorned every wall and there was a quiet calmness to the place that spoke of the genteel people of the past.

Gabe checked them in as Claire took in her surroundings.

'Our luggage will be in our rooms shortly. Do you want to freshen up before we head out?' Gabe asked. Claire nodded, still unable to quite take it all in and together they climbed the staircase.

★   ★   ★

Their first stop was York Minister. Claire had been there before but it seemed the most impressive place to start their tour. Gabe seemed very taken with the city and its quirky charm. They stood outside the Minster and looked up. The choir were practising and the sweet music was drifting out of the main doors which had been pushed open.

There were groups of tourists everywhere, some with guides holding up umbrellas or flags to keep their tour group together, and others in pairs, all of them taking photographs. Claire could identify French and Spanish but there were a multitude of other languages being spoken.

'Let's go inside and look round,' Gabe said. Claire nodded and looked at him closely. His words were hurried as if he needed to get away from something. He didn't look at her but instead seemed to be scanning the groups of people.

Gabe started to walk away from Claire and so she hurried to catch up. She had no idea what was going on but it was clear that she wasn't going to get any answers standing outside. They walked through the massive doors, into the dim interior. Here and there on the stone floor coloured light played as the sun shone through the stained glass windows.

Gabe seemed to momentarily forget whatever was bothering him and looked up to the Great East Window. Claire followed his gaze. She had seen it before but it had not lost its magic, each smaller window depicting a different scene.

The magic was broken a little by the sound of loud American voices behind them. Other tourists turned round to give disapproving glares but Claire saw Gabe stiffen and start to walk towards the window and away from the crowd. Now Claire was officially suspicious. What on earth was going on?

'Gabe?' she said softly as she caught up with him.

'This was a mistake. We shouldn't have come,' he said and his voice carried an accusation.

Claire took a step back, almost feeling as if she had been slapped in the face. Gabe looked at Claire. His expression softened and then crumpled into an apology.

'I'm sorry. I didn't mean it like that.' He shook his head as if he didn't know how to explain to her. 'Please, let's go.' Gabe took hold of her hand and whisked her into one of the smaller side chapels.

'If we just wait here a minute and then we can leave.' Gabe was peering out of the chapel, clearly looking for someone. But who it was, Claire had no idea. The odds of him meeting anyone he knew here must be astronomical. And yet Gabe was acting as if he was been stalked by a crazy person.

Gabe reached for her hand again and Claire allowed herself to be pulled along, her mind too busy coming up with increasingly unlikely explanations for Gabe's behaviour.

They were almost back at the main

doors when Claire heard the shout.

'Gabriel McKenna!'

It was almost more of a scream than a shout but Claire didn't have time to turn and see who it was. Gabe was dragging her along at such a pace that she had to run, or else be pulled over.

The Price of Fame

Claire was out of breath and starting to feel scared and more than a little cross. Gabe was pulling her along, not checking to see if she was all right.

They wove in between the crowds and every now and then Gabe would look over his shoulder and run faster. They were on the other side of the small city and there were fewer people here.

Claire started to slow up and managed to free her hand from Gabe's. She wasn't going a step further until she knew exactly what was going on. The most logical explanation she had, however unlikely, was that one of Gabe's ex-girlfriends had somehow tracked him to York.

She came to a stop and stood with her hands on her hips, her breathing coming in fast, ragged gasps. Her feet hurt, her thin soled sandals not designed for running and she was feeling hot and windswept.

'What . . . is . . . going . . . on?' she managed to squeeze out between breaths.

Gabe had stopped too, although the look on his face suggested that he wanted to keep running.

'I will explain but not here, not now.'

'Gabe, this is ridiculous . . . ' Claire started to say but running feet sounded behind her and she didn't argue when Gabe grabbed her hand and pulled her into a small café. But instead of stopping and sitting down, maybe even getting a drink, he pulled her past the counter and out into the kitchen at the back.

'Hey!' the owner shouted. 'What do you think you are doing?'

'Sorry, bro!' Gabe shouted but the words were probably lost as they burst through the back door and out into a yard that ran behind the row of shops. Gabe had a tight grip on Claire's hand

and now she was starting to feel frightened. What exactly was Gabe running away from? To make him behave like this, it couldn't be anything good.

Gabe led them out of the yard and on to a smaller side street. A taxi whizzed past and Gabe held up his arm but the taxi kept going.

'Why didn't he stop?' he said, pulling Claire down the pavement.

'Because you have to book him. He's not that kind of taxi,' Claire said. 'If you want a cab you'll need to go to the taxi rank.'

Claire was pulling on Gabe's hand again, to slow him down. There were no shouts or sound of running feet. Whoever they were running from, were gone, for now at least. The taxi that had whizzed past was now parked up in a spot down the road. Gabe walked towards him.

'I'll give you fifty pounds if you'll take us to The Principal Hotel,' Gabe said to the woman through the open window. The woman stared at him, as if she didn't believe him and so Gabe pulled out his wallet and handed over the notes.

'Hop in,' she said.

Gabe pushed Claire in first and then climbed in beside her as the driver pulled out into the traffic.

'Now will you tell me what's going on?' Claire asked, turning to Gabe but he had pulled his phone from his pocket and seemed engrossed in the screen. Claire glared at him but he either didn't notice or didn't care. Claire could not believe that handsome, kind and funny Gabe had turned into . . . whatever this was.

She was beginning to wish she had come to York alone. She felt as if Gabe had burst her happiness bubble and wondered if the rest of the trip would be marred by his strange behaviour.

Since he was ignoring her, she decided the best thing to do was to ignore him right back. He was the one behaving so oddly and so he could be the one to explain and apologise. She stared out of the window as they drove down streets lined with Victorian and Edwardian large properties and tried to imagine who lived there now, letting her imagination run free to try and block out what had just happened.

'We'll need to collect our luggage and find somewhere else to stay,' Gabe said, although whether he was talking to himself or Claire, it wasn't clear.

Claire said nothing. She had no idea what you say to a comment like that. Had he been trying to impress her with the fancy hotel and beautiful rooms? Was this all just a ploy because in reality he couldn't afford them? No, that didn't seem right, either. She let out a sigh of frustration.

'Look, Gabe, it's fine. I can find a room at a bed and breakfast. So I'll get my bag and head off and then you will be free to do whatever you want.'

She had his full attention now but wasn't sure she wanted it. He looked hurt and confused, which she thought accurately mirrored her own feelings.

'I'm not sure what on earth sort of game this is . . . ' Claire started to say and then stopped. Henry would never be friends with someone who played games like that and he would certainly be upset that Gabe was doing whatever it was that he was doing.

'It's not a game,' Gabe said, his voice suddenly edged with a quiet fury.

'Then what is it?' Claire countered, allowing some of her anger to show. 'One minute we are having a great time, seeing the sights and the next you are dragging me half way round York, as if you were being chased by your mortal enemy.'

The taxi driver had taken the turn for the hotel and slowed down.

'Must be someone famous staying,' she said in a thick Yorkshire accent. 'If you're lucky you might get to spot them at dinner.'

Claire looked out the front windscreen and could see a small group of young women had gathered outside the hotel. A few were jumping up and down and most of them had their phones out and were taking photographs but Claire couldn't see any target. Beside her, Gabe slid down in his seat.

'Take us somewhere else,' Gabe said. 'Anywhere else.'

The taxi driver looked over her shoulder at Gabe and then shrugged as if it didn't make much difference to her. The taxi travelled past the group of young women and kept going. At first Claire was sure they were going to ignore the taxi but one of the women turned round and started to scream, jumping up and down and pointing at the taxi.

'They must think we are the . . . ' Claire started to say and then she saw Gabe's face. She didn't know how or why, but it had just become clear that the group of screaming women seemed to think that he was the famous one.

'You?' Claire squeaked.

'Unfortunately, yes,' Gabe said, as if it were the worst thing in the world.

'But what for?' Claire asked, wondering why Henry had never mentioned that his friend was famous, at least at home. She had noted that the screaming voices had sounded American. Her mind raced as she imagined that he was an infamous criminal or maybe a politician but none of those things seemed to match up with what she knew about Gabe, or perhaps what she thought she knew about Gabe.

But then, she asked herself, how come he seemed to have so much money? How come he was able to take six weeks away from work in a country that was notoriously stingy with holiday allowance? What was it that he wasn't telling her? She stopped looking out of the window and leaned back in her seat.

'I'm an actor,' Gabe said in the kind of way that one might admit to working for the tax man.

'OK . . . ' Claire said, still not sure how that explained things but she felt like it was a piece of the puzzle.

'I've always done theatre before. This really hasn't been my experience.'

'Wait . . . those people are fans?' Claire almost laughed at herself. She had come up with a range of crazy explanations but she had never thought that Gabe was being chased by fans. That somehow felt even more far-fetched.

'It would appear so. I filmed a new TV show in the autumn and it seems to have been a runaway success.'

'That's brilliant,' Claire said, but feeling a bit dazed by the new information.

'It's one of the reasons I asked Henry if I could come over for the whole summer, instead of for just the wedding.'

Now Gabe sounded miserable and Claire wasn't sure what to make of it. If he was an actor then surely he would be happy to have fans. I mean that was all part of the deal, wasn't it? Especially if you wanted your TV show to continue.

'I know you must think I am being a

bit of a diva,' Gabe said and he was looking at Claire now, as was the taxi driver, via her rear view mirror.

'Well, no, not exactly but I have to admit that I thought the fan thing was all part of it.'

'It is,' Gabe said with a shrug, 'but I have spent the last few months not being able to go out. I mean not even to the grocery store. Everywhere I go, everyone I'm with, I get followed and I just needed a break.'

For a few moments Claire tried to imagine what it would be like to have people follow you everywhere, taking photos and recording every aspect of your life. She shivered at the thought.

'That must be difficult.' Claire glanced out of the front windscreen and caught the taxi driver's eye. Clearly the driver thought that all that money would probably make it worth it.

'I never expected it to be like this. I mean I knew there might be fans but they camp outside my house and the paparazzi try to take photos through the windows.' Gabe ran his hand through his hair.

'Really?' Claire couldn't imagine that level of invasion of privacy and she had to admit it sounded awful.

'I just wanted a few weeks of going unrecognised. I mean, the TV show isn't on in the UK and I thought it would give me some time to figure it out. But if they know where we are staying then the press won't be far behind. I'm sorry.'

Claire shrugged.

'The hotel was lovely, don't get me wrong, but I was expecting to stay in a B and B, so there is really no need to apologise. How about we find somewhere to stay outside of York? I'm sure they won't track you to somewhere small and discreet.'

Claire flashed her eyes to the rear view mirror but the taxi driver studiously kept her eyes on the road. That could be a problem, she thought, as would retrieving their luggage.

'Can you take us to the station?'

Claire asked the taxi driver.

'Of course, love,' the driver said but she was obviously a little disappointed that she wouldn't get to drive them to their final destination, which Claire was in no doubt she planned to share.

Claire looked at Gabe and he seemed to understand her message and so they fell silent as the driver took them round the one way system and back to the station.

Worlds Apart

They climbed out of the taxi and this time it was Claire taking Gabe by the hand and leading him through the station. They stopped at a ticket machine and bought tickets. Claire looked at the station electronic signs and then started to run. They made it to the platform just in time and found seats on the train, which was half empty.

'Scar — borough?' Gabe said.

Claire smiled.

'I know the perfect place for you to hide out. I'm sure no-one will guess that you've headed there and I doubt there will be hordes of American tourists who might recognise you.'

Gabe returned her smile, for the first time since the Minster and Claire felt a wave of relief. It seemed like the old Gabe was back but a tiny part of her mind asked the question. Which was the real Gabe? The famous TV star who ran from fans or the charming, friendly, relaxed man she had come to have feelings for? She pushed the question from her mind.

What mattered now was getting away to somewhere secret. Then she could figure out what all this meant.

'So what's in Scar-borough?' Gabe asked in that American way of breaking down words into more syllables than was necessary.

'A really nice little B and B. I used to come here with my family in the summer holidays. I know the owners well and we can ask them not to confirm we are here, should anyone ring up and ask.'

Gabe nodded and he seemed to relax.

'It's not exactly what you're used to but is comfortable and homely.'

'Sounds perfect,' Gabe said with a grin. 'And are you going to show me the delights of the town?'

'Oh yes. Traditional seaside resort. You're going to love it.' Claire did. It held fond memories and even now, years later, took her back to some happy times. Scarborough was one of those places that never seemed to really change, as if were stuck in a different era.

The only flaw in the plan would be if Jeff and Tina were fully booked, which of course they were, it being the summer holidays, as Claire discovered when she pulled out her phone to ring them. But they did have a place that she could use, if she didn't mind it being on a static caravan site.

Claire readily agreed, without speaking to Gabe, knowing that they were probably lucky to get that. Jeff and Tina kept the caravan free for family to use and thankfully none of their many children were using it for the next few days.

Claire kept her eyes from glancing at Gabe. She wasn't sure that she wanted to see what his reaction to their new accommodation would be. She thought it would probably be much like her own when they arrived at the hotel, but for entirely different reasons. She didn't think any Hollywood star had ever stayed at the Sunshine and Showers Caravan Park.

Most of the static caravans were close enough together that you could comfortably have a conversation with your neighbour. In fact, you could probably hand a cup of tea from one window to another. None of the residents seemed to mind, most had kids and the traditional boundaries of different properties didn't seem to apply.

Claire had picked up the key from the small reception, which also functioned as a shop, and was now leading Gabe down the path that led through the centre of the park, past the children's play area and into a fenced off area that contained the individually owned static caravans.

Jeff and Tina's was right at the far end, with a lovely view of the sea. She walked up the steps to open the door and found memories of long ago summer holidays flooding her mind. She smiled to herself as she remembered how excited they used to be and how she and her sister would argue over whose turn it was to unlock the door.

It was hot inside, with all the windows closed and so Claire quickly moved through and opened the windows, letting in the sea air. At last she felt ready to face Gabe. What she feared most was that he would pour scorn on a place that was part of her most treasured childhood memories.

'Wow, look at that view,' he said and Claire could see he was transfixed by the ever changing blue of the sea and the horizon.

'Tina and Jeff got first dibs when this place was built so they got to pick their spot,' Claire replied, walking to stand next to him so that she could check out the view. 'When we first came to Scarborough we would stay in the B and B but when my mum and dad got to know Tina and Jeff, they started to offer us this place.'

Gabe nodded but his face was unreadable so she couldn't tell what he was thinking.

'I don't think anyone will recognise you here,' Claire added tentatively.

'It's perfect, Claire, thank you.'

Gabe sat down on the U-shaped sofa and Claire took a seat opposite, with the table in between them. It was as if they were attending some kind of board meeting.

'Why didn't you tell me before?' Claire asked. It was a relief to know that he wasn't hiding anything like a wife or girlfriend but at the same time, she couldn't really understand why he couldn't have just told her what he did for a living — or why Henry hadn't told her, for that matter. She planned to give Henry a piece of her mind, next time she saw him.

'The last six months have been crazy,' Gabe said slowly as if he were choosing his words carefully. 'I had no idea that my life would change so much.' He shook his head as if he couldn't quite believe it himself.

'But isn't part of being an actor, becoming famous? Isn't that all part of success?'

Gabe's face showed a flash of anger but it was quickly suppressed. Claire had seen it, though, and the doubts started to rise to the surface again. Did she really know Gabe? The real Gabe? Or had he just been acting out the part of 'normal bloke'?

'You're right, of course. But not so much if you stick to theatres. You get the occasional fan wanting an autograph at the stage door but that's about it.'

'So why did you take the part?' Claire assumed that the money had been good and she couldn't help hoping money wasn't the reason. She wasn't sure why. Of course you needed money to live, but to take a job simply because of the money and for no other reason, well, that made Gabe a different person to the one she thought she knew.

'It wasn't the money,' Gabe said hurriedly which gave the impression he had been asked that question before and was worried that people would think that was his motivation.

'Then why?' Claire asked, when it seemed that Gabe wasn't going to speak of his own accord.

Gabe ran his hand through his hair.

'A buddy of mine was trying to sell a pilot to the network and he said he would have more chance of being heard if he had a 'name' attached to the project. He's being working so hard to get a breakthrough and I didn't feel I could say no. I was supposed to appear in the pilot and that would be it but the network saw the scenes that were shot and said yes, but only if I committed to the whole series.'

Claire nodded. She had no real understanding of how Hollywood worked but it kind of made sense.

'So you didn't really have a choice?'

Gabe leaned forward so that his

elbows were on the table and he stared down at his clenched fists.

'Not unless I wanted to trample all over my buddy's lifelong dream. The script was good, really good, and I knew that he might not get a second chance. I couldn't let him down.'

'So fast forward six months and the show *is* a great success but now you have a collection of stalker fans.'

'A rumour started going around that I might not sign up for year two and since then, I feel like I haven't had a moment's peace.' He looked up at her now. 'Then Henry suggested I come over to Scotland. The first season isn't going to be shown here till after Christmas. Not that it means it will automatically become a success.' Again his words came out in a hurry but this time as if he was worried that Claire would think he had a massive ego. She smiled at him.

'I get it. I just wish you had told me earlier.' She kept her smile in place but a small voice in her head was questioning what else she didn't know about Gabe. For all she knew he could have a famous actor girlfriend at home.

'I know I should have — I just didn't know how you would react. Or even if you would believe me.'

Claire could feel his eyes on her, studying her closely.

'And how do you feel now?' he asked and Claire turned to look out to the sea. She knew it was a mistake as soon as she did. She didn't need to say anything to him. She had given away her feelings by her actions, despite the fact that she wasn't even sure how she felt about Gabe's revelation.

'OK,' Gabe said and stood up. 'I get it.' He made a move towards the door.

'Where are you going?' Claire said. She didn't know what she was feeling but she knew she didn't want Gabe to go.

'It's clear you don't want me here.'

'I never said that,' Claire said, leaping to her feet. 'But you have to admit, that for me at least, today has been a little surreal. You never talked about what you did for a living and now you tell me you're this famous actor, who gets followed around by photographers and crazy fans.'

'I didn't think I'd need to tell you.'

Claire stared at Gabe, her mouth open a little.

'And if I had asked you direct, what would you have said?'

Gabe shrugged.

'Things were going so well that I guess I would have just made something up.'

Claire found herself mouthing the words 'made something up'.

Gabe made a frustrated noise.

'I just wanted you to get to know me, before I told you . . . ' But Claire cut him off.

'How could I get to know you, if you were planning to lie to me about this clearly important part of your life?' She knew the anger she felt wasn't just directed at Gabe. She was cross with herself for letting her imagination carry her away to a place where love was simple and the only thing she thought she had to worry about was how far apart they lived.

She now realised that the physical miles weren't the problem, but their lifestyles were a million miles apart. There was no way she could ever fit into his life and she suspected he would be deeply unhappy if he tried to fit in to her mundane existence.

'This was what I was afraid of. That you wouldn't be able to see past all that.'

'I guess you'll never know, now,' Claire said, folding her arms across her chest. She felt like she needed to protect her heart for what was coming next.

'If you won't even let me explain then I think I should go.'

'Perhaps you should,' Claire said, equally stubbornly. Despite the angry words, she didn't want him to go, not really. If they could both calm down then maybe they could talk things through like grown-ups. But what was the point? They clearly had no future together, so better to stop now before she invested more of herself.

'I really like you, Claire. I'm sorry that you couldn't see a way to at least give this a go.'

Claire opened her mouth to defend herself, to tell Gabe that he was being unfair but he was gone before she could find the words. He closed the door firmly behind him and she watched him stride off into the distance.

She felt for the seat behind her and crumpled into it, before curling up into a ball and letting the tears flow.

Nothing More to be Said

When the knock came at the door, Claire had no idea how much time had passed. She had fallen asleep curled up on the sofa and now the sun was setting across the bay.

She scrambled to her feet and wiped a sleeve across her face, hoping that sleep had erased the trail of tears. Claire yanked open the door, half expecting to see Gabe standing there asking if they could talk but instead it was Will, Jeff and Tina's son.

Will worked in York and Tina had arranged for him to pick up Claire's case from the hotel and bring it to her on his way home. As far as Claire was concerned, Gabe could sort out retrieving his own luggage.

Will was dressed in the uniform of a supermarket. He looked tired and so Claire simply thanked him for picking up her bag and watched him walk away, no doubt looking forward to a few beers with his mates after a long week.

Claire dumped her bag on the small table and then went looking for food. Jeff and Tina kept the caravan well stocked with staples. Claire didn't think she could face having to make conversation at the shop, so she settled for a cup of tea, made with long life milk, making a mental note to ensure that she replaced it before she left.

What she needed to do was get her act together. She had a wedding to go to tomorrow and now that she wasn't staying in York, she would have to think about train times and getting up early.

★   ★   ★

Claire was almost the last to arrive at the church. She nipped inside just as the bride's car drew up at the front entrance. The church was full and so Claire found a seat at the back, which she was quite happy to do.

The last thing she felt like doing today was going to a wedding. Her friends would all be in a party mood, celebrating the happy couple and all Claire wanted to do was be alone, so she could be miserable in peace. The only good thing that could be said was that at least Henry and Jen wouldn't be there. Which would of course mean that there was no chance of her having to see Gabe.

The church service was beautiful and both Catherine and Glen had beamed as they took their vows. Normally Claire would have beamed with them, but instead she had to fight back her tears. People cried at weddings but there was a significant difference between tears of joy and the tears that were threatening Claire. She knew she had to hold them back. If she didn't she would break down and sob as the anger and sadness leaked out of her.

She didn't know why she felt this way. She had known Gabe all of a few weeks and the sensible part of her brain had told her all the way that there was no chance for them, however her traitorous heart might be feeling.

He lived on the other side of the world, and now that she knew he was a famous actor there was no way that he could be interested in her. But if that were true why had he reacted so strongly? He had seemed genuinely hurt that she had been wrong-footed by both his revelation and the fact that he had kept it from her.

But were an actor's emotions ever truly genuine? After all, he must be able to summon all sorts at will to be a decent performer. No. She shook her head. Any possible relationship had been doomed and now that she had a taste of a summer fling, she didn't think she liked it. There seemed to be heartbreak waiting at every turn.

Claire had been by herself for some time and been content. There was no reason she couldn't do that again, assuming she could rid her mind of all the images of Gabe. Gabe smiling at her. Gabe laughing. Gabe reaching for her hand. The congregation stood as the vicar announced that Catherine and Glen were now husband and wife and Claire forced herself to smile and clap as they shared their first kiss as a married couple.

Catherine had become a friend when they had shared a placement together at a very challenging school. They had been firm friends ever since and the least Claire could do was celebrate her friend's happiness.

Outside the small church the congregation gathered and Claire waited for an opportunity to go and say her congratulations, as the photographer took some family photos. At one point she caught Catherine's eye and her friend gave her a small wave, her face alight with happiness.

'Claire?' a voice said behind her. Claire went stock still. Her mind raced as she realised who it must be. She did her best to compose herself. She wasn't ready for this. She knew that she would likely see Gabe at the next wedding but that was a whole week away. A week she had planned on coming up with a strategy of how she would deal with the inevitably awkward situation. She couldn't deal with this now, not here, not so publicly.

'Claire?'

Around her, people were beginning to look in her direction and she was in danger of making a scene. The last thing Claire wanted. She didn't want to bring any kind of drama to Catherine's wedding. Her friend deserved better than that. So she forced herself to turn around and face him.

Gabe's face looked as anguished as her own. He was a few steps away from her and looked as if he was afraid to come any closer. Claire, aware that a few curious stares were still aimed in their direction, started to walk away from the crowds. Gabe followed her but kept his distance.

When Claire thought she was far enough away from the action she stopped. A quick view of the crowds told her that they had turned their attention back to the bride and groom.

'What are you doing here?' Claire said, so softly that she wasn't sure he would hear her words.

'I couldn't sleep,' Gabe said and Claire frowned. That didn't seem to be much of an explanation for tracking her down and arriving uninvited at a stranger's wedding.

Claire forced herself to look him in the eye. Despite her makeup, she knew that she looked tired, too. He nodded as if he had received the wordless message loud and clear.

'I mean, I couldn't leave it as we did.'

'You left,' Claire said. She knew she needed to keep her answers to a minimum. The raw emotion was barely being held at bay and if she got into a deep discussion with Gabe, she knew she would not be able to hold it back. What she needed was time to process.

'I thought it was for the best . . . ' Gabe said but Claire interrupted him.

'Perhaps it was but if you believe that why are you here?'

'I made a mistake. I shouldn't have walked away. We should have talked about it some more.'

He looked wretched as he ran his hand through his hair and Claire felt her resolve waver. If they were both so unhappy then perhaps they *should* talk. Gabe glanced behind him and scanned the street. Claire shook her head, it was all she needed to be reminded of all that had happened the day before. No, there was no hope for them. Better to end it and deal with the heartache now. Better that than a few short weeks of a sort of happiness that would only end.

'I'm not sure there is anything to talk about,' Claire said, flinching as she saw the pain of her words cross his face.

'Gabe,' she said more gently and she waited until he was looking her in the eye, 'there can be no future for us, surely you can see that. We are worlds apart, literally and figuratively. Better to agree to be friends now, than simply delay the heartache that will be there waiting for us both at the end of the summer.'

'And if I don't agree?' he said, his eyes flashing.

'If we can't agree then I'm not sure there is anything more to be said.'

Claire turned as she heard her name being called. Catherine was gesturing for her to come and she saw the photographer looking a little impatient. One of her other friends, Ben, was making his way towards her.

'I have to go,' she said as she turned back to Gabe, but Gabe was gone. She could see him walking stiffly away down the street. And in that moment she was sure she would never see him again.

Heart to Heart

Sunday morning and Claire took the train home. She had been planning on travelling around Northumberland before the next wedding in Durham but now all she wanted to do was to escape back to her own place.

She dumped her bag in the hall and then went and threw herself on the bed. Usually she loved being away all summer but once she had watched Gabe walk away from her all she wanted was the comforts of home.

She had smiled and laughed her way through the wedding reception and had been impressed with her own ability to act but now that she was home, all she wanted to do was sleep and then she needed to work out how she was going to face Gabe at the next wedding.

The week seemed to fly past as only weeks in the holiday can. Claire stayed mostly at home, reading books she had been meaning to read all year and ordering takeaways. It was almost like a self-imposed retreat. Except that she was pretty sure retreats were supposed to allow you to find answers to dilemmas, and Claire had found none.

When she thought of Gabe all she could see now was the hurt on his face and it was almost unbearable. But she couldn't shift the nagging doubt that perhaps it was all an act. He was, after all, an actor who could pretend to feel all kinds of emotions. Maybe he had just wanted a summer fling and Claire had ruined his plans?

She shook her head as that thought crossed her mind once more. If she had been going on the Gabe she knew before York, it would never have occurred to her. But now she wasn't sure she knew him at all. Why hadn't he simply told her, from the start, what he did for a living? It was difficult to know now, how she might have reacted. But it was possible it could have saved them both pain, as she doubted she would have ever considered Gabe as anything other than a summer friend, one who she might send Christmas cards to but who she was unlikely to see ever again.

And so for the third weekend of Claire's summer holiday she found herself getting ready for another wedding. She had caught the fast train to Durham and this weekend, accommodation had been provided — assuming that you considered tents a form of accommodation.

Claire was due to meet Henry and Jen at the train station in Durham and they had agreed to get a taxi together to the site of the wedding, in a field outside the city centre. All the way up on the train, Claire practised her 'we are just friends' approach and could only hope that she would be able to pull it off in front of Henry and Jen, who knew her well.

They had arranged to meet outside the coffee shop at Durham station and Claire caught sight of Henry and Jen waiting for her. They both had ruck-sacks laid at their feet but Claire couldn't see Gabe. She felt instant relief which quickly became a kind of sadness that she couldn't explain.

Gabe hadn't come and she shouldn't have been surprised. Even without what had happened between them, she could imagine that Gabe could only cope with so many strangers' weddings.

'Claire!' Jen said, waving once she caught sight of her. Jen ran over and pulled her into a quick tight hug. 'It's good to see you.' Jen released Claire and gave her an assessing eye. 'How are you?' she asked more seriously and her words were hurried as if she wanted to ask before Henry was in earshot.

'I'm fine, Jen,' Claire said, forcing a smile on her face as she wondered how much Jen knew. 'Really,' she added when she saw the look on Jen's face.

'Henry doesn't know but I sort of guessed. We'll talk later, I promise,' Jen said as they walked over to where Henry was guarding the bags.

'Claire! Good to see you again,' Henry said as he pulled Claire in to a hug. 'Gabe decided to sit this one out. Don't blame the man. There is such a thing as too many weddings.' Henry was smiling and Claire was fairly sure he had believed whatever excuse Gabe had come up with. Jen looked at her knowingly and Claire nodded slightly to indicate that yes, they would talk about this later, when Henry wasn't around.

'Henry! Weddings are a beautiful thing,' Jen said in a voice that sounded as if she was telling him off, but with great affection.

'They are usually, but this one is a Wicca ceremony in a field. Who gets married in a field?'

'Apparently Tam and Adrian,' Claire said, giving him a wry smile. She wasn't sure what to expect either but she was also relieved that this wedding at least, had no formal element to it. In fact the dress code had been listed as 'clothes not required' but Claire was fairly sure that was Tam's idea of a joke. Or at least she hoped it was. She was planning on wearing an ankle-length, flowery dress that she had bought in a small second-hand vintage shop near home. As soon as Claire had tried it on she thought it would be perfect for the occasion and go well with the circlet of flowers that all the women would be wearing.

The camping turned out to be more like glamping. The tents were in fact huts that were spacious and contained comfortable looking camp beds and had fairy lights hung from the vaulted ceilings. Claire was sharing a hut with Jen and Henry and even Henry seemed impressed with what he was seeing. Outside there was a bar, bonfire and a barbecue and as soon as Jen got the chance she sent Henry off in search of some of his mates.

'So,' Jen said as she handed Claire a chilled glass of wine and sat down in one of the many deckchairs that had also been provided. 'Are you going to tell me what happened between you and Gabe?'

Claire took a sip of wine and smiled in satisfaction. This was definitely more of what she had in mind for her summer holidays.

'I thought you knew,' Claire said, wondering if there was any way to avoid this conversation. For the first time in over a week she was feeling relaxed and she could feel the stress start to melt away. The last thing she wanted was to reawaken all that pain.

'Let's say I made an educated guess. Gabe wasn't very forthcoming.'

Claire nodded as she took this in.

'How is he?' she asked, not sure she wanted to know the answer.

'Miserable. Brooding,' Jen said, taking a sip of her own wine.

'Well, he is an actor,' Claire said. She didn't want to come out and ask if Jen thought his emotions were real and this seemed the safest way to do that without actually voicing the accusation.

'Ah,' Jen said knowingly.

'Ah?' Claire asked.

'So he told you?'

'He didn't really have much choice. What with the hordes of pretty women chasing us down the street.'

'Oh. Well, that certainly explains his mood. He was hoping for six weeks away from the craziness.'

'It certainly was crazy,' Claire said, wondering if his mood was simply the fact that his life in America seemed to have found him on holiday.

'He's really struggling with it,' Jen said and Claire could feel her studying her closely but she kept her eyes fixed on all the activity in the field.

'Can't be easy,' Claire said non-committedly.

'Henry will be back soon. Are you going to tell me what happened or what? It's clear that you were both developing a thing for each other.'

If Claire hadn't felt like crying she would have probably laughed. Jen was renowned for getting straight to the point in the bluntest way possible.

'We were but what was the point? In less than four weeks he will be back living the Hollywood life and I will be back at school teaching small children. Surely you can see the miles between us aren't the only issue.'

'All that stuff can be overcome if you love each other.'

Now Claire did laugh but it was without humour.

'Come on, Jen. We aren't in some kind of romantic comedy. Real life doesn't work like that.'

'It does if you want it to,' Jen said.

They sat in silence for a few minutes.

'And just in case you might be interested, I think Gabe wants to be with you. So the question is whether you want to be with him.'

Silence

The wedding ceremony had been short and sweet, and supposedly blessed by Mother Earth. The party afterwards had been great fun — almost enough for Claire to forget the words that Jen had spoken. What Jen didn't know was how important trust was to Claire. In fact it was what she needed most in a relationship, especially one with the odds stacked so firmly against it.

As Claire lay on her camp bed staring up at the fairy lights strung across the roof, it was almost as if she were outside, sleeping under the stars. And she couldn't help wondering what Gabe was doing and whether he was thinking of her as she was of him.

Despite what Jen had said, Claire couldn't shake the feeling that the relationship would be doomed from the start and if she felt heartache now, how much worse would it be at the end of the summer? But was that her problem all along? Was that why she was still by herself when so many of her friends were getting married and settling down? Had they all had to take a leap of faith of some kind?

The real question, of course, was whether Claire would be prepared to do the same. Despite her adventurous travel, she had never been one to risk her heart.

It was strange that she could have such polar opposite elements to her nature. And she still struggled with the fact that Gabe had hidden that part of himself and only revealed it when he had been forced to. But if Jen was right and that part of his life drove him crazy maybe the person she had met at the airport in London was the real Gabe.

Claire closed her eyes and tried to focus on something else, tried to get some sleep but the questions would not be silent. And so she made her decision.

In the morning she would ring Gabe and suggest that they meet somewhere to talk.

Claire sent the text and waited but her phone remained stubbornly silent. Perhaps she had left it too late. Perhaps too much hurt had been dealt out and Gabe was making the decision for her. Maybe, for him, at least, it was already over. She rolled on her side and hugged her knees.

She had no-one to blame but herself. She had thrown away a chance of happiness. And that's what she realised it was. There were no certainties in life and sometimes you had to take a chance. A chance that she hadn't been willing to risk and now she was receiving her reward. Claire turned her face into her pillow as the tears came. The last thing she wanted to do was wake Jen and Henry. The last thing she wanted to do was have to share how foolish she had been.

★ ★ ★

The next morning there was to be a communal big breakfast before the bride and groom left for their honeymoon and the rest of the guests made their way home.

Claire woke to the smell of bacon and sausages being cooked on the line of barbecues which had been used to cook the meal the night before. The last thing Claire felt like doing was going out and being sociable but she knew that trying to avoid it would only result in more questions. Questions that she wasn't ready to answer just yet.

She didn't bother looking at her phone. What was the point? Gabe had made his thoughts clear by not answering her text when she had sent it. He always had his phone on him and he had never delayed answering her before now so it seemed obvious that not answering was in fact his answer.

Claire freshened up and got dressed. There was no sign of Jen and Henry so she assumed that they had already headed out for breakfast. And despite the fact that the night had ended in the early hours, Claire was surprised how many guests had made it to breakfast.

A table was set up with glasses of chilled orange juice and urns of coffee. There were piles of plates and signs directing them to the meat barbecues and the vegetarian ones.

When Claire had first woken up she didn't think she could eat a thing but now that she was outside, her stomach seemed to rumble. She took that as a good sign. She was sure that people with broken hearts lost their appetite. If she had regained hers then surely that meant she was already recovering?

She grabbed a plate and a roll before helping herself to bacon and a sausage. She was liberally splashing it with tomato ketchup when she heard Jen calling her over to one of the blankets that had been laid out on the grass.

'Morning, Claire,' Henry said with a grin. He looked a little tired, with bags under his eyes but also blissfully happy. He and Jen had spent a lot of the night before dancing and Claire was sure they were both wishing their own wedding would come sooner than the last week of the summer holidays.

'Morning,' Claire said and she managed a smile.

'Could you get me a coffee?' Jen said, taking one look at the expression on Claire's face. Apparently Claire had managed to fool Henry but Jen was not so easily taken in. 'Do you want one, Claire?' Jen asked.

'That would be lovely,' Claire said, sitting down cross-legged as Henry stood up.

'You have about two minutes to tell me what happened,' Jen said and there was a hint of urgency in her voice.

'Nothing really. I texted Gabe and he made it clear that it was over.'

Jen managed to look both shocked and stricken.

'Claire, I'm so, so sorry. I would never have encouraged you to contact him if I thought he would behave like that.'

Claire couldn't bear to see her friend upset and so she reached over a hand and gave her arm a squeeze.

'For one thing, it's not your fault. You have no control over how someone else behaves and second, I know that you just want the best for me.'

'I do . . . ' Jen started to say but Henry had reappeared with three cups of coffee.

'You OK?' Henry asked Jen, carefully kneeling down and handing out the hot drinks. His look of concern nearly made Claire cry. His concern showed such love in a simple query and Claire knew that was what she wanted in her life, too. Perhaps she could have had that with Gabe. To push down the sob, Claire took a sip of the too hot coffee. It burned her lips but at least it was a distraction.

'I'm fine, just tired and sad that we aren't going to see Claire again till the wedding.'

'That is a shame. You sure we can tempt you back to Edinburgh before the big day?' Henry said, turning his attention from his soon-to-be wife back to Claire.

'I have my summer planned out,' Claire said, once more managing to find a smile from somewhere, 'and besides, you and Jen will have your hands full. The wedding is only a few weeks away now.'

Jen, of course, knew the real reason that Claire would not come to Edinburgh but she wasn't about to share that with Henry.

'Exactly — and Claire needs to enjoy her holiday. It's bad enough that she has to spend every weekend going to a different wedding, not to mention the fact that she helped Lorna pull hers off at the last minute. Claire deserves a break.'

Jen smiled at Claire and Claire nodded back, relieved that Jen had managed to come up with a reason that Henry could believe.

Claire needed some time to get her head and heart back together, and there was no way she could do that in Edinburgh. Planning someone else's wedding whilst trying to avoid the man who had broken your heart was not a recipe for healing.

Claire had planned to stay in the north of the country for the following week but it felt too close to Gabe. It was ridiculous, she knew there was no way she was going to bump into him but still . . . She felt the need to get as far away as possible.

She travelled with Henry and Jen to the train station and waved them off as their train took them north. Claire had no idea where she was going to go and so stood and stared at the departures board.

There was one train that caught her eye. A direct train to Exeter and from there she could head into Cornwall. She couldn't get much further away unless she decided to leave the country altogether. Without giving herself time to debate whether this was a good idea, she hurried to the ticket machine and bought the ticket.

As she climbed on the train, she switched off her phone. A week of silence seemed exactly what she needed.

Now That I've
Found You . . .

Cornwall was as beautiful as Claire knew it would be but it was also incredibly busy. It hadn't been easy to find a place to stay. Usually she would have booked way before the summer holidays but this had been a spur of the moment decision and that was why she had had to go out and buy a cheap two man tent, a sleeping bag and a one ring gas burner.

It wasn't as luxurious as the glamping at the wedding but it had a certain simplicity to it that Claire found was what she needed. Claire loved children, but after one trip to a local tourist attraction, full to the brim with stressed-out parents and hyperactive kids, she had decided that she needed to avoid them.

Instead she had visited a local charity shop, stocked up on books and found a cliff top site that was quiet and away from the crowds and spent most days with a picnic lunch and a good book.

There were no romances in her pile of books, and so instead she read old-fashioned murder mysteries and biographies.

It was idyllic and as long as Claire pushed the memories of Gabe away she found she could get through a day without tears. Crying about it wasn't going to change anything, she told herself firmly. She would see Gabe again in less than two weeks at Henry and Jen's wedding and she needed to be able to be around him without breaking down. That wouldn't be fair on Jen and Henry or anyone else for that matter. She wasn't a teenager, after all.

Sitting outside her tent, crossed-legged on a small blanket and eating her supper of pasta — there were only so many dishes you could conjure up on one ring of gas — Claire watched the children playing football. She smiled as all the older children let the younger ones join in and she was reminded of happy days at the holiday park in Scarborough.

Her smile dropped a little as more recent memories of Gabe striding away from her, filled her mind. A shadow crossed her and she looked up. She couldn't make out who it was, as the sun was behind them, but from the size she knew it was a grown-up.

Claire put down her bowl of pasta and raised a hand to shield her eyes and then she knew that her mind was playing tricks on her. It couldn't be. She had just been thinking about Gabe walking away from her, so angry and hurt, and now he seemed to be standing before her but she knew it couldn't be. She had told no-one where she was going and had resisted the temptation to even switch her phone on. She looked away and blinked, sure that the apparition would disappear as quickly as it had appeared.

'Hello, Claire,' the shadow said and Claire forced herself to look back. To imagine seeing Gabe was one thing, but to hear him speak? She was sure now that this was no trick of her mind.

'Gabe!' she exclaimed, not knowing what else to say. 'What are you doing here?' she added dumbly, the first thing that came to mind.

'Looking for you,' he said mildly, as if tracking her down to a campsite in Cornwall was nothing. He sat beside her, leaning back on his arms with his legs stretched out before him.

'How did you find me?' Claire squeaked. Her heart was thumping fast in her chest, now that she knew it was real, now that she knew he was really here. It was impossible but yet here he was. And not only that, he was acting like it was no big deal.

She looked at him as he shrugged and she felt the familiar tug of frustration. Was this going to be another thing that he refused to share? Gabe was staring at her now and he seemed to read her expression.

'I was worried. You didn't reply to any of my texts or my calls. Jen and Henry had no idea where you were. I even went to your apartment but you weren't there, either.'

'I needed some space . . . to think,' she added reluctantly.

'I get that but why would you send me a text and then not wait to hear a reply?'

'I did wait!' Claire said indignantly.

'I replied as soon as I woke up,' Gabe said mildly and Claire felt her cheeks redden. She had sent the text long after midnight and then switched her phone off as soon as she got on the train. Had she really not given him the chance to answer?

Of course now it all made perfect sense and Claire felt like a fool. Why had she expected Gabe to respond straight away? Why hadn't she considered that there was a perfectly reasonable explanation for his lack of response? Thinking that getting no response was his answer, now seemed ridiculous.

'Oh,' Claire said. What else could she say? If she tried to explain it she would only sound slightly crazy. But Gabe was smiling at her which told her that he had guessed at least some of the reasons behind her behaviour.

'And then I got worried. No-one knew where you were and you weren't answering your phone.'

Claire thought she could detect some reproach in his comments, which she thought was unfair. He had walked away from her twice, so why was it such a big deal that she had done the same? The flash of anger was there and then it was gone. He had travelled across a whole country to find her, because he was worried. That said something about him as a person and not only that, maybe what he felt for her. She frowned.

'How did you find me?' she asked and was greeted with silence. When she looked up from her close study of the grass in front of her, she realised that Gabe was looking anywhere but at her.

'Gabe?' she asked again. No more secrets, she told herself. Not if they were going to see where their relationship might go.

'You'll laugh. Or you'll get angry. It's probably evens on which.'

'I'll get more cross if you don't tell me anything,' she said. She had no idea how he had tracked her down and his unwillingness to answer was starting to nip at her.

'I hired a private eye,' he said, again focusing on the children's football match in front of him.

Claire stared and then she laughed.

'Really?' she squeaked once she managed to find breath between giggles. 'A private detective? I didn't know we even had those!'

'You do in London,' Gabe said and he had switched his attention from the match back to her but his face said he still wasn't sure how she was going to react.

Claire's eyes went wide both at the thought that Gabe had actually hired one and the fact that she had been tracked down so easily.

'Look, I know it probably seems a bit over the top. Even a bit stalker-ish. But I was worried, so was Henry and when you weren't at your apartment . . .'

Claire took this in. She hadn't really thought about that. Her mind had been focused simply on the efforts he had gone to, to check that she was OK.

'I just started imagining that something bad had happened . . .'

'I'm sorry,' Claire said. 'I hadn't really thought it through and when I didn't hear from you . . . I just jumped to my own conclusions, I guess.'

'What are we like?' Gabe asked and this time he was grinning.

'We aren't doing very well on the trying to understand each other,' Claire added.

'And I'm sorry about that,' Gabe said and he had lost his grin. 'My life has been so crazy this year. And when I met you, it seemed like I could get my old life back but then all the craziness in York. And I know I hurt you, Claire. I didn't mean to. I just ... ' Gabe seemed to have run out of words and Claire reached for his hand and gave it a squeeze.

'I'm sorry, too. I really like you, Gabe, but I was worried that we would both get hurt. Our lives are so different. I'm not sure how we could ever make it work and then I got a taste of your life and well ... I couldn't see myself coping with that.' Claire squeezed Gabe's hand again. She didn't want to hurt him but she knew she needed to be honest.

'I understand,' Gabe said his voice heavy. 'Well I'm glad you are OK, Claire.' And he pulled his hand away and stood up.

'Where are you going?' Claire asked.

'I needed to know you were OK and you are. We needed to talk and I think we have said all that needs to be said,' Gabe said, brushing grass from his chinos. He smiled but Claire could see it was a great effort. 'My life isn't going to change any time soon. I've signed a contract for another two seasons. I wish I hadn't but I have and you're right, our lives are so different. I hate the scrutiny and I would never ask you to take that on too. I like you too much to ask you to do that.'

Gabe leaned down and kissed her gently on the forehead. Claire was still trying to take in all he had said. Why had he signed on for more, when he hated it so? She remembered what he had said about his friend, but even so. To give up two more years of your life? That seemed too much for anyone to ask of a friend.

'Goodbye, Claire,' Gabe said and once more Claire was left watching Gabe walk away from her.

Hope for Tomorrow?

Claire stood on the platform of the train station in Edinburgh, looking for any sign of Lorna and Jack. They were back from their honeymoon and had offered Claire a place to stay as she attended her last wedding of the season, Henry and Jen's.

A couple appeared through the crowd and Claire knew it was them. Jack had his arm thrown around the shoulders of his wife and Lorna was waving madly. They were both grinning like the cat that got the cream.

Claire couldn't help smiling to see them so happy, especially after all the drama before the wedding. If any two people in the world deserved to be happy, it was Lorna and Jack. But there was a part of her that was glad the summer was nearly over. In some respects it had been the best summer ever, full of hope and promise, but now all Claire could really think about was the heartache.

And she longed for the rhythm of term time and work, where she was sure she would be able to forget all that had happened.

Lorna pulled her into a tight hug. Claire had debated telling her what had happened but decided against it when she caught sight of Lorna's blissful expression. Lorna deserved to be happy, particularly after the upset before the wedding and Claire wasn't going to be the one to break the spell.

Lorna took half a step back but didn't release Claire. Claire smiled, and it was genuine. It was wonderful to see her best friend, and to see her looking so content. But it was also clear from Lorna's expression that she had used her particular powers to pick up on the fact that something wasn't right.

'It's so good to see you!' Claire said with great enthusiasm, which she meant but she also hoped might keep the conversation away from her. 'How was Paris?'

'Well, we have over a thousand photos to show you,' Jack said with a grin. He was renowned for taking lots of photos.

'And the wedding photos are in,' Lorna said with a broad grin.

'I can't wait,' Claire said.

'Well, Jack is going out with his mates tonight so we can have a takeaway and a proper catch-up.'

Jack pulled Lorna into him and gave her a kiss on the forehead as if he wasn't quite ready to let her go, even if a night out with his mates was on offer.

Claire felt a pang of sadness. That's what I want, she thought to herself. I want someone who wants to be with me, like Jack does with Lorna, but who knows me well enough to give me space when I need to catch up with friends. Aware that Lorna was looking at her thoughtfully, Claire laughed.

'Sounds good.' Perhaps it would be good to talk to Lorna. Claire hadn't really spoken to anyone about how she felt since she last saw Gabe. Jen had texted, of course, although Claire had no idea what Gabe had told her, so all that Claire had said was that she and Gabe had talked and parted as friends. This was after all the truth, even if it did not give away her feelings on the matter.

'I won't be late,' Jack said, kissing Lorna one last time.

'Just have fun,' Lorna said, 'and don't worry about what time you get back. We'll probably still be up.'

Jack nodded and it was only when Lorna gave him a little push that he finally went out of the door. Lorna closed it behind her new husband and then turned to face Claire.

'Right, now you need to tell me exactly what is going on,' Lorna said in that voice that brooked no nonsense, or any suggestion that she would accept anything other than the full truth of the matter.

Claire sighed from her position,

flopped on the sofa and took a sip of wine.

'Are you sure you wouldn't rather tell me all about your honeymoon?' Claire said with one last stab at avoiding the conversation.

'That's all we've talked about all day, Claire,' Lorna said sternly. 'Now it's your turn.'

'But I don't want to kill the mood.'

'I'm sure it's not that bad,' Lorna said and then Claire's face crumpled as if all the walls she had built to hold back the emotion crashed down all together.

Claire wasn't sure how long she had cried, as her friend held her close, but she wouldn't have been surprised if Jack had reappeared before she had finished. In reality it was only about half an hour and Claire had to admit that she felt better having a good cry.

'Right,' Lorna said, 'I'm going to order the takeaway. You top up the wine and then you are going to tell me everything from the beginning.'

It took two glasses of wine, the takeaway and some chocolate that Lorna had found for pudding, for Claire to explain all that had happened with Gabe. Saying it out loud made it seemed even harder to believe and it seemed to Claire that they had never really been on the same page, at least not at the same time. The all-too-familiar doubts rose up again. If you loved someone, then you made it work, however hard it was, didn't you?

'How do you feel about it now?' Lorna asked, bringing in two mugs of coffee.

'I really don't know but I'm not sure it matters. Gabe seems to have made up his mind.'

Lorna raised an eyebrow and Claire knew Lorna well enough to know that she was not convinced by her last statement. Claire shrugged.

'In such a short period of time we have been back and forth on the issue of how different our lives are that I feel like I've got whiplash.'

'Exactly!' Lorna exclaimed triumphantly. Now Claire frowned. She couldn't see how that was a good thing.

'Claire, there is clearly a spark between you, something that keeps you both coming back for more, despite the odds as you see them. That means something.'

'Having the ability to make each other miserable?'

'You wouldn't be miserable if you both didn't have feelings for each other. And he hired a private investigator to find you because he was worried about you.'

'You don't think that was a bit over the top?' Claire asked, watching her friend closely for her reaction.

'Completely!' Lorna said but she was smiling. 'That's exactly the kind of reaction someone has when they are hopelessly in love.'

Claire felt the familiar sense of warmth and hope burn through her but it was quickly followed by its partner, hopelessness, the knowledge that it was all for nothing and that the only result had been a broken heart.

'Exactly, its hopeless. I've waited so long to feel like this. To meet someone that I could imagine spending the rest of my life with and then fate pulls a trick like this.'

'Claire,' Lorna said and this time her stern voice was back, 'the only thing that can truly separate two people in love is one of them dying.' Lorna fixed Claire with her best 'listen up' look. 'You and Gabe need to talk about this. It's clear you are both miserable being apart. If you really want to, you will make it work.'

'Lorna, he's famous. I mean we were actually chased by a group of beautiful women! What could he possibly see in me?'

'Everything he has ever wanted, I expect,' Lorna said in a voice that told Claire she wasn't about to listen to Claire put herself down.

'We live on different continents,' Claire said.

'Well, thankfully he's a TV star who could probably afford a private jet.'

'I'm not sure that I'm a private jet kind of person.'

'Are you going to let that stand between you and the love of your life?' Lorna was indignant now and Claire couldn't help but smile at her friend's reaction.

'No, but I'm really not sure that Gabe feels the same. The last time we talked he seemed pretty set on ending it.'

'Well according to Jen he is as miserable as sin.'

'You spoke to Jen?' Claire was incredulous.

'Of course I did, when you were freshening up. I knew something was going on and I guessed it might have something to do with the handsome American.'

'Gabe's miserable?'

'Putting a good face on it, apparently, just like you, but anyone with half a heart can see through it.'

Claire didn't know what to say to that. She hated the thought that Gabe was hurting like she was, but at the same time it did make her wonder if Lorna was right.

'So at the wedding tomorrow, you are both going to sit down together and talk about it and if needed I will come and referee.'

Claire's eyes went wide at the thought.

'I don't think that will be necessary,' she said hurriedly.

Lorna's eyebrow shot up.

'From what I can see, you two have failed to tell each other how you really feel on multiple occasions. I have a feeling my services might be required.'

Claire winced and Lorna's expression softened.

'OK, I'll let you have a go first but I'll be close by and will step in if needed.'

Claire nodded. Maybe they did need help — although it had the feeling of when she had to step in between two of her class, who were friends but were arguing.

Despite it all, Claire felt butterflies in her stomach at the thought of seeing Gabe again. Unbidden, her mind started to imagine the life they could have together, if only they could make it work.

A Promise of Happiness

Despite the late night, Claire was awake early. There was no sign of Lorna or Jack and so Claire made herself a cup of tea and went to sit on the small balcony off the lounge that gave a great view of the city.

She was trying to picture talking to Gabe and sorting everything out, but each time she tried, the memories of their previous conversations seemed to smother everything. They had this one last chance.

Claire knew that Gabe would be heading back to America shortly after the wedding and it was much harder imagining how they could sort out their feelings when such a distance stood between them.

'Thinking about Gabe?' a voice said behind her. Claire jumped a little at the unexpected sound and then blinked in surprise when she realised it was Jack.

'Lorna told you,' Claire said, more of a statement than a question.

'She did, I hope you don't mind.' Jack took the other seat and placed a plate of chocolate croissants on the table.

'Of course not, we're friends, too. Even if it is all a little embarrassing.'

Jack smiled.

'Love makes us fools,' Jack said as Claire smiled. 'Did I ever tell you how I nearly messed it up with Lorna?'

Claire's eyes widened. Jack mess things up with Lorna? She would have found it easier to believe Jack if he was telling her that the world was flat. Lorna had certainly never mentioned it.

'I was due to meet up with Lorna one night after school and Lorna cancelled at the last minute. Said something had come up and could we reschedule. I said of course but something didn't sit right. Lorna normally told me everything and I had the feeling she was keeping secrets. It drove me crazy to the point that I thought I had to go out and find her.'

Claire raised an eyebrow.

'I know, I know, believe me,' Jack said, running his hand through his hair at the memory. 'Not my finest hour, but still.'

'You found her?'

Jack nodded.

'With her arm around another man. I watched as I saw her pull him into a hug. Not a 'we're just friends hug' but a proper one, you know?'

Claire nodded.

'Then I knew I needed to be anywhere but there and so I ran, afraid that Lorna would see me but more afraid of what I had just seen.'

Jack took a sip of his coffee and his eyes showed that he was lost in the memory.

'The next day I met up with Lorna and she didn't say anything about it and I couldn't bring myself to ask but it was eating away at me. I started to feel angry and hurt, even though I had no idea what actually was going on. Lorna knew something was off and kept asking me but I got angrier and angrier. I guess I kind of felt like she should know why I was so upset.'

Jack shook his head at the thought.

'Anyway. Eventually one of Lorna's friends mentioned Mike, a guy who was having a really tough time, I mean really tough, and how Lorna had dropped everything to get him the help he needed.'

Claire nodded. That sounded like Lorna.

'I felt like the worst kind of idiot. I had let doubt creep in and let my worst fears interpret her behaviour. I was lucky that I hadn't done anything foolish that meant I lost Lorna for ever.'

Jack looked at Claire and she could see he was trying to tell her something, she just wasn't exactly sure what.

'I guess what I'm trying to say is that you need to talk to Gabe, really talk and listen to each other. It sounds as if you both have kind of assumed you know what the other is thinking . . . ' Jack stopped as if he was afraid that he might have gone too far but Claire knew that he was right. She reached out a hand for his arm.

'I think you're right, but Gabe does a lot of walking off when the conversation gets uncomfortable.'

'Well, it's a good job I told him the same thing last night,' Jack said with a grin.

Claire looked shocked. She couldn't help it. It didn't seem like the kind of conversation that Jack would be comfortable having.

'In case you're wondering,' he said standing up and stretching, 'it was Lorna's idea.'

Now Claire smiled, of course it was. No wonder she was so keen for Jack to go out with his mates.

'Morning,' Lorna said, appearing in the lounge in her pyjamas. 'We ought to start getting ready. We don't want to be late.'

Henry and Jen's wedding was at the small church near Jen's parents, in a village outside the city. Claire, Lorna and Jack walked up the long path that snaked through the beautifully kept churchyard up to the wooden door. Standing outside was Henry, looking more excited than nervous, and Gabe, who looked distinctly nervous.

Claire couldn't help smiling at the sight of Gabe in his kilt and jacket. He looked the part as well as simply gorgeous.

Henry and Jack shook hands and hugged and Lorna kissed Henry on the cheek. Which left Gabe and Claire staring at each other. Claire tried out a tentative smile and Gabe returned it with a look of relief. Then Gabe leaned in to kiss Claire on the cheek.

'I'd like to talk later, if you don't mind.'

Claire didn't trust herself to speak. She felt like her insides had just been through the spin cycle of a washing machine and her heart was leaping all over the place in her chest. So instead she nodded and smiled and Gabe seemed to take that as a 'yes'.

Gabe showed them all to their seats a few rows from the front and as they sat down, Lorna reached for Claire's hand and gave it a squeeze, accompanied by a knowing look.

Jen looked stunning as she walked down the aisle. She wore a simple lace dress with her family tartan as a sash and her father grinned as if he was the luckiest man alive. The service was beautiful and both Henry and Jen cried as they said their vows. In fact Claire was fairly sure there wasn't a dry eye in the house.

Since Gabe was in most of the photos, Claire had an opportunity to stand back and watch him. He had a lovely way with people and it was mainly due to him that the photographs were taken quickly and without the usual hour or two of the other guests having to stand around.

A row of classic cars arrived to take the bridal party and close family to the reception venue and then a 1940s bus arrived to take the other guests.

The barn on Jen's family farm was decked out with flowers in purple and white and fairy lights and the guests walked through an arch of white roses into the great hall.

The round tables were set at one end with the long table on the raised platform at the other end. Behind the platform Claire could already see the traditional Gaelic band setting up for the ceilidh that was to follow the meal. When the bride and groom entered, a cheer went up and then the feasting began.

Claire's face was starting to ache with the smiles and laughter by the time Gabe stood up to do his best man's speech. It was funny and touching and spoke of his great friendship for Henry and his affection for Jen.

'And I think we can all agree that

there is no truer pair in all of Scotland. Those of us who remain single can only hope that Cupid's arrow will be so kind.' Gabe's eyes were fixed on Claire as he raised his glass of champagne and the hall stood as one and did the same.

'To the bride and groom!' he shouted and the hall replied.

Throughout the feast that followed, Claire could feel Gabe watching her. She was so desperate to speak to him that she could only pick at her food.

The promise of future hope and happiness was almost too much, particularly when she was surrounded by other people's 'happy ever after'.

If Lorna noticed that Claire had hardly touched her food, she said nothing, as if she knew what Claire was feeling and that to talk about it would only make things worse. Claire felt like she was standing on a precipice and she would either soar or fall.

Finally the remnants of the meal were taken away and the guests were invited to go outside and stretch their legs whilst the tables were moved to make room for the ceilidh.

Claire was one of the first outside, desperate to find Gabe, but as she stood with Lorna and Jack and a group of the other friends, all she could do was keep an eye on the door and wait for him to appear.

But Gabe didn't appear. Claire knew that he was probably helping set up but a small part of her felt like he was avoiding her. They needed to talk but perhaps Gabe was putting off having to tell her finally, once and for all, that it would never work. If that was the case then Claire was sure she didn't want to have that conversation either. What was the point? That had all been said before.

When the Caller stood on the steps to the barn and invited the guests to return for the dancing, that Henry and Jen were to start, Claire had decided the best thing to do was to join in with the dancing.

If Gabe didn't want to speak to her,

then she was sure they could continue to avoid each other for the evening. And then after that? Well, after that, Gabe would go back to America and she would return to her life in London.

A Decision is Reached

Claire stood and watched Henry and Jen dance. It was clear they had practised. Henry was focusing so hard on the unfamiliar steps that he wore a look of concentration throughout which only made Jen laugh.

Once their solo was over, the Caller invited the best man and maid of honour, Jen's sister, Heather, to join and then the respective parents.

Claire smiled and clapped along with the others, determined not to let her emotions show. This was a happy day and Claire wasn't going to ruin it by having some kind of teenage heartbroken breakdown.

In truth, nothing had really changed. When she had arrived back in Edinburgh, she had her plan and although her hopes had been raised again, she knew her friends were just trying to do what they felt was best.

Jack may have been right, that she and Gabe should talk, properly talk, but that advice was only good if you were both on the same page.

The dance finished and then the rest of the guests were invited to take part in a reel. Claire joined in, despite the fact that she could see Gabe standing in line at the far end. The way the dance worked she knew she was likely to work her way up to him, but their meeting would be brief and there would be no opportunity to speak.

Despite how she was feeling, Claire couldn't help pick up the laughter and fun around her. By the time she had swirled into place opposite Gabe, she was pink-cheeked and smiling.

Gabe grinned back at her as he swung her around and Claire felt dizzy. Not just from the energetic spins but the shift in her heart. This day was turning out to be as up and down as a rough sea crossing. When Gabe gave her hands a firm squeeze, before releasing her to her next partner, Claire was sure that Gabe wanted to speak to her as much as she had wanted to speak to him earlier.

As soon as the dance was over she excused herself from the next one, on the premise of needing some fresh air. She tried to catch Gabe's eye but he was involved in a lively conversation with some of Henry's friends from work. All she could do was hope that Gabe would notice that she was missing and come and find her.

There were small groups of people outside, laughing and drinking, taking a break from the dancing and enjoying the cool evening breeze but Claire moved away from them to find a quiet spot.

A few picnic tables had been set up outside and Claire picked the one furthest away from the barn and sat down, waiting. Claire listened as the band finished another dance. She felt nervous as her hands didn't seem to want to stay still. She wasn't sure what was worse — the waiting or the anticipation of what Gabe might have to say.

Claire had cooled down to the point that she was starting to feel the chill when Gabe's kilted figure appeared at the barn door. He moved between the groups, stopping to say hello, before he finally spotted her in her lonely spot. His eyes were fixed on her as he made his excuses and headed her way.

'Claire,' he said and then took a seat beside her. 'I had no idea how involved my best man duties were going to be.'

She smiled at him to show she understood, despite the fact that she had been waiting for him in the cold. Gabe noticed that she was shivering and unbuttoned his jacket, before slipping it around her shoulders.

'And now I've left you shivering in the cold.' He sounded concerned.

'It's fine. I was hot after all that dancing.'

'I was a little sceptical at first but it's kind of fun. And between you and me I had a few lessons with Henry's mum so I didn't look the fool.'

'You looked the image of a Scottish gentleman.'

'Why, thank you, lass,' Gabe said in his best attempt at a Scottish accent, which made them both laugh.

'So . . . ' Gabe said.

'So?' Claire replied.

'Would I be right in thinking you had the same pep talk from Jack that I did?' Gabe's eyes were more solemn now as if he knew how important their next conversation would be.

'If it was the one about talking and listening, then yes,' Claire said, feeling her breath catch slightly in her throat.

Gabe nodded and they both seemed scared to speak.

'Why don't you tell me what you are thinking?' Claire asked, knowing that it was a bit cowardly to ask him to go first.

Gabe nodded again and Claire detected the same reluctance that she felt. She wanted to know what Gabe was thinking but only if it was in line with her own thoughts. If it was another rejection she didn't think she could face it but also knew that love came with risk. It was all so confusing.

'I know it's been a bit of a whirlwind. Our time together,' he added as if he needed to explain. 'And I wish I had been upfront with you from the start. I guess I was just hoping you would like me, the real me . . . I was trying to escape from my life, maybe even the 'new' me.' Gabe made inverted commas with his fingers.

Claire reached for Gabe's hand and gave it a squeeze. She didn't want to interrupt him but at the same time she wanted to let him know that she understood. She had been hurt by the fact he had kept such a large part of his life from her but now she also understood why he might have felt the need to do that.

Gabe looked from their interlinked hands to Claire's face and smiled. Claire smiled back. He had got the message and so far neither of them had walked away from the conversation hurt. Maybe this would be easier than she thought.

'My life in the US is crazy and I know I should be more grateful but it's just not me, you know?'

Claire nodded sadly. Would this be the crux of the matter? If Gabe felt like a fish out of water in his own life then there was no way she would ever fit.

'So I've made a decision.'

Claire tried to swallow down the lump that had suddenly appeared in her throat and blinked furiously to keep the tears that threatened at bay.

She couldn't blame him if he decided that there was no future for them. If he made that decision he was most likely trying to protect her from the life that he didn't enjoy and that she wouldn't either.

'I understand,' she said when it looked like Gabe couldn't find the words to say what he needed to.

Gabe was shaking his head.

'Don't say that. That is how all our previous conversations have been. We both assumed we knew what the other was thinking without letting them say it.'

There was an edge to his voice and Claire tried not to take it to heart. He was talking about both of them, she told herself firmly, it didn't mean he was blaming her.

'The thing is, Claire . . .' he started to say but his words were interrupted by a loud shout. They both looked up as a taxi van drew up outside the barn. Gabe frowned and then his expression turned stormy. Men and women poured out of the van and they were all laden down with expensive looking cameras.

'Gabriel!' one of the women shouted, turning her lens in his direction as soon as her feet hit the ground.

'Give us a smile, mate!' a man yelled, as Gabe got to his feet.

'Is this your summer fling?' another shouted.

Gabe pulled Claire to her feet and spun her round, using his arms to shield her from the flashes of the cameras.

'This is private property. And you all need to leave right now,' Gabe said and Claire didn't think she had ever heard him so angry.

'How did they find you here?' Claire whispered, not sure that Gabe would be able to hear her over the clamour from the journalists and photographers.

'No idea, I've been off social media,' Gabe rumbled back. 'Let's go back inside,' he said and started to move Claire in the direction of the barn but the group seemed to swarm in front of them and their way forward was blocked.

Claire kept her eyes closed and her face turned into Gabe's chest. She couldn't believe what was happening and could only imagine what Gabe's life was like back in the US. One thing she did know was that it wasn't for her. She couldn't imagine being trailed everywhere she went by photographers. What would her school say? What about the children? Surely she would be left alone at work? They couldn't be that interested in her, could they? But Claire knew the answer. She had read enough stories about people being hounded by the media. It was too much and all she wanted to do was run away and hide. She could only imagine how Gabe felt.

There was a loud bang and Claire covered her ears. She had no idea where the sound came from but she could see the swarm of journalists move back a little. Claire uncovered her ears and heard a familiar voice, in a thick Scottish accent.

'If you'll be kind enough to be leaving ma land promptly, I'll not fill you with buckshot.' It was Jen's father, who held his shotgun crooked over his arm. His tone was mild but sure.

The journalists had moved a little but not enough it seemed. Jen's father cocked his gun.

'Trespassers are asked to leave nicely

once. I dinnae think you want to be around if I have to ask ye again.'

If Only . . .

This seemed to be enough for most of the group who started hurrying back towards the taxi. The driver had seemed to get the first message and had reversed the van back up the track to the entrance from the road. One or two seemed prepared to risk it but as soon as Jen's father pointed his gun in their direction, they scurried away as if they had a pack of dogs chasing at their heels.

'Well now, lad, you should be left in peace for the rest of the evening,' Jen's father said with a smile.

'I'm sorry to cause you such trouble,' Gabe said.

'Nonsense,' Jen's father said, throwing an arm around Gabe's shoulders. 'You've nothing to apologise for. Unless you invited them?' Jen's father added with a grin when he saw Gabe's expression.

'No, sir, they're never invited.'

'I thought as much. Now you and lovely Claire are to forget about them and enjoy the party. We Scots never let anything stand in our way when a celebration is to be had.'

Jen's father slapped Gabe on the back and then marched back off into the barn. A small crowd had gathered at the doors to see what all the fuss was about but quickly rejoined the dancing when it appeared the excitement was over.

Gabe and Claire stood looking at each other, as though they were on an awkward first date and had run out of things to say to each other.

'I'm sorry about that,' Gabe said, managing to look both sorry and cross at the same time.

'Not your fault,' Claire said automatically although a small part of her did wonder how they had been found. Was Gabe protesting too much? Was this all part of some kind of plan? She pushed the thought away as soon as it appeared.

No, that didn't fit with what she knew about Gabe and she had to hold on to that, to trust that. She knew enough about the gossip mags to know that they would go to extraordinary lengths to get their story and there were plenty of people, the caterers, the photographer, and the car drivers who could have sold their story.

Gabe sighed and it forced Claire to look at him.

'What?' she asked, still distracted by her thoughts of who could have leaked Gabe's location. Was this what it was like for him? Questioning everyone in his life, constantly wondering who he could trust? She didn't think she could bear that.

'You,' Gabe said, running a hand through his hair and taking a step away from her.

'Me?' Claire said, feeling as if she had woken up halfway through a conversation and now had no idea what they were actually talking about.

'I can see your mind whirring,' Gabe

said shaking his head. 'And I can take a guess at what you are thinking. You are wondering if I told the hacks where I would be as some kind of play for publicity.'

Claire blushed, there was no hiding the truth when her body was so ready to give it away.

'I was,' she said slowly but then Gabe turned away from her and she reached out to grab him by the arm, 'for about two seconds.' That made Gabe pause and Claire gently squeezed the arm that she held. 'Then I started wondering who might have leaked the story.'

Claire watched as Gabe's shoulders sagged a little.

'And then I thought how awful that must be. Always wondering who you can trust. Wondering who might betray you if the money was high enough.'

Gabe turned to face her and Claire could see that he was assessing her reaction. He wanted to know if what she said was the truth or if she was just saying what she thought he wanted to hear. Before today she would have got cross, probably said something that she would later regret and then walked off. But now she had a better idea of what his life was like, so instead she stood there and looked at him evenly.

Gabe nodded and Claire moved towards him so that she could reach for his hand. She took it in hers.

'I thought I understood what your life was like but in truth I had no real idea. Now I think I do, it was just a few moments but I think I understand now.'

Claire stood on her tiptoes and reached up to kiss him.

'I'm sorry,' she whispered when they finally broke apart from their kiss. Gabe raised an eyebrow. 'I had no idea, not really,' she added.

'You shouldn't feel sorry for me, I did this. I live in that world. I knew what I was getting into.'

'You did it for your friend,' Claire said simply with a smile.

'Did I, though?' Gabe said and once

more he looked tortured. 'That's the story I keep telling myself but what if that's not true? What if I'm just protesting now because I don't like it? The money is good, Claire. Really good. What if I sold out my life and my theatre career because of the money? I keep asking myself that question.'

Gabe started to pace and Claire let him. She wasn't shocked at his words. She could understand how he might doubt his own motives. People might claim that they weren't motivated by money but if you had lived on very little, like she had as a newly qualified teacher, trying to live in London, she knew almost anyone could be tempted.

'I keep asking myself how different this situation would have been.'

'What do you mean?' Claire asked softly, although deep down she knew what he meant. It was something she had thought about a lot since she had found out about his occupation. What if they had met and he was a theatre actor and she was a teacher? Would it have been easier? More straightforward to consider a future together?

She hated to admit it but she had a feeling the answer would have been yes. She had tried not to let herself dwell on that alternative universe, one where it would have been so simple to be together.

Perhaps Gabe could have worked in London — they weren't exactly short of theatres. She could meet him after each performance and they could go out to eat.

Claire dug her fingernails into the palm of her hand. None of those thoughts or dreams were helpful. They had to deal with the reality, not wish that things were different. Wishing wasn't going to change anything.

'It might have been different,' Claire conceded. She didn't want to focus on that, it was too painful, like a shattered dream. 'But we need to think about the here and the now.'

'I just wish . . . ' Gabe started to say but then one look at Claire stilled that sentence. 'You're right,' he said clenching his fists by his side. 'Whatever my motives, I made that decision and others since. I have to live with them.'

Claire nodded. In that moment she didn't trust her voice not to break with the overwhelming emotions. Was Gabe about to tell her that it was hopeless? That they couldn't focus on what could have been? That he couldn't ask her to live the life he had chosen?

'The question is . . . ' Gabe said, reaching for Claire's hand, 'is it something you could live with, just for the next couple of years?'

For Ever and Always

Claire had braced herself for this. No, she shook her head, not for this. She had prepared herself for Gabe to tell her that their worlds were just too far apart. Not just geographically but everything else. She had expected him to say that he would never ask her to step into his world, to give up all semblance of privacy and to walk away from the life she had known.

'I understand,' Gabe said, releasing her hand and taking a step back. 'Really, I do. If I'm honest I wouldn't wish this on my worst enemy. It's like having a permanent shadow. All your best moments and your worst end up in the public domain, however hard you try.'

'No, you don't understand,' Claire said, not bothering to keep the edge of anger from her voice. They were not going to do this again.

'I think I do,' Gabe said sadly.

'Let me finish!' Claire said, stamping her foot. Gabe looked surprised but there was also the twitch of a smile on his face. Claire ignored it. She couldn't be distracted by how handsome he was or how charming. She needed to tell him what she really thought. Right now. Gabe held both hands up as if surrendering.

'You always jump to conclusions,' she said crossly. 'For once can you keep quiet?'

Gabe opened his mouth but closed it again firmly and then childishly put a finger over his lips. Claire glared once but then forced herself to focus. This was too important.

'I've thought about this a lot.' She paused and looked at Gabe, as if she were daring him to interrupt her but he simply nodded. There was less humour now and she knew he was going to listen to what she had to say.

'And you're right — our worlds are

far apart.' Gabe nodded and the humour was all gone now, only resignation showed on his face. 'But the question I keep coming back to is — does it matter?'

Gabe's eyes went wide but he said nothing.

'I've spent all summer watching my friends get married, finding their own happiness. And what I've learned is that every relationship faces challenges, whatever they might be. But in spite of that, or maybe because of it, all of them have taken their leap and decided, one way or another, that it is worth the risk.'

Now Claire started pacing, as if she needed the movement to keep her words flowing.

'That's always been my problem, you know. I've never been a risk taker. I've always preferred the safer option. The one where I could predict the outcome.'

Claire looked at Gabe and had to hide her grin at how desperate he obviously was to say something. She took a deep breath and kept going. If she stopped now she would never say what she needed to.

'But then I met you.' Gabe's eyes danced but he said nothing. 'And that changed. For once in my life I thought about taking a risk. A risk on a relationship that all statistics tell me is doomed. You live in America and I live here. I know you won't move here and I couldn't see myself walking away from teaching so that was the first problem but still I let myself ... ' Claire frowned. Was she really going to say those words out loud? 'I let myself fall in love with you.'

Claire turned away from Gabe. She didn't want to see his reaction to the words. Not until she had finished.

'I did. I felt like I knew you, even though it had been a matter of days and then there was the big bombshell. A whole part of your life that you hadn't shared. I felt like I didn't know you at all. I mean, how could you keep something like that from me?'

She risked a look now and Gabe's

finger waved on his lips. Claire held up a hand.

'I came up with all sorts of explanations, most of them not good and then there was this evening. We were going to meet up and talk, really talk. No-one storming off until we had talked it all through. But then your life crashed in on it again and we never got to finish.'

'Claire . . . ' Gabe said but one look silenced him.

'I thought that was it, that was the end of it but then I knew I understood for perhaps the first time. I got a glimpse of what your life was like. What you must think about. How you must worry about who to trust and I got it. I understand, Gabe.'

Claire stopped talking and looked at Gabe, really looked at him. Together they seemed trapped in the moment, lost in each other's thoughts. Claire tried out a smile and Gabe returned it with his own, but there was pain in his eyes and Claire knew that she needed to keep going, to push through her own fears and tell him how she felt.

'What I'm trying to say is that I understand your life now and that doesn't change how I feel about you.'

Claire's statement hung in the air between them. Gabe seemed to be trying to comprehend the words she had just said. Claire waited but when Gabe said nothing, her confidence started to slip. What if he had intended on telling her that it couldn't work, that his feelings weren't strong enough for him to want to try. She could feel the embarrassment burn up her chest to her face and she had to look away. To hide how she felt.

'Claire?' Gabe's voice was soft as he reached for her. 'You really are the most amazing woman.'

'It's OK, I understand,' Claire replied, moving out of reach.

Gabe chuckled and that made Claire pause.

'Now who's not letting the other finish?'

She forced herself to look at him. He had his hands on his hips and one eyebrow raised and she didn't think he had ever looked more handsome.

'Sorry,' she mumbled as the words came out all wobbly, a reflection of what her insides were doing at that moment. Gabe reached for her hand and this time she let him take it. He pulled her to his chest and Claire allowed herself to dissolve into his hug.

'Are you going to let me finish?' he murmured into her hair.

Claire nodded, not trusting herself to speak and hoping that this wasn't just a dream.

'I said, before I was interrupted . . .' He paused and Claire giggled. She didn't know where it came from but there it was. Despite all the turmoil she was feeling, he could still make her laugh.

'You are the most incredible woman I have ever met.' Gabe's voice had gone husky as if he was having the same difficulty controlling his emotions. 'And I love you.'

Claire felt Gabe's arms tighten around her and she knew that she would do whatever it took to be with this man. This man who loved her and who she adored back. She would give up her privacy and her life as she knew it to be with him, because this was love and it was worth the risk.

'But . . . ' Gabe said and Claire felt like a balloon that had been popped. She pulled herself away from him. She needed to see his face. He looked serious and Claire didn't think she could bear it. To go through all they had, for her then to make that decision and then for Gabe to . . .

'I can see your imagination is running away with you again,' Gabe said and he was smiling again. Claire frowned.

'Well, perhaps you could lose the drama and just say what you need to.'

Gabe chuckled.

'You're right, as always. What I was

going to say is that you need to be sure. I will do my best to keep you out of the spotlight but it seems inevitable that someone will pick up the story.' He was serious again. 'You need to be sure, Claire. I hate that part of my life and I don't want to make you have to live with it, too.'

'Do you love me?' Claire asked, reaching for his hand and looking him in the eye.

'Yes,' Gabe said, his voice a little hoarse. 'I've never felt like this before but you have to understand, Claire, that's what gives me pause. Part of me knows that if I truly love you I should let you go, at least until this chapter of my life is over.'

Claire shook her head.

'You have been to how many weddings this summer?' Claire asked. Gabe looked confused at the sudden change in conversation but she could see he was mentally totting them up.

'Four if you include this one.'

Claire smiled.

'And at any of them, did you listen to the vows?'

'Yes,' Gabe said and Claire thought he had started to catch up.

'The bit about sickness and health, richer for poorer, for better for worse?'

'I did, but this isn't really the same thing.' Gabe said and Claire raised an eyebrow.

'Isn't it? When I was listening to Henry and Jen say their vows I thought of our situation. If you love someone, you put them first, you take them as they are, not how you wish them to be and so what I am trying to say . . . ' Claire paused to take a deep breath. 'Is that I love you and I take you and your crazy life as part of that.'

Gabe seemed lost for words, which Claire hoped was a good sign.

'Do you mean that?' he said at last, his eyes bright with emotion.

'I do,' Claire said simply. 'I love you, Gabriel, and I want to be with you and we will figure out the rest as we go along. If you'll have me?'

'Are you kidding?' Gabe said, simultaneously sweeping Claire up into his arms. 'I love you, Claire, with all my heart. I would move heaven and earth for you. If you'll have me and all the craziness that follows me around.'

'For ever and always,' Claire managed to say as her head spun and her heart felt like it was going to burst.

'For ever and always,' Gabe whispered back as he spun her around under the Scottish stars.

The Hollywood Wedding
of the Year?

'So the question is, are you ready for the Hollywood wedding of the year?' Lorna said to Claire as she gently fixed Claire's veil.

'Oh, stop it.' Claire groaned. 'Do you think we've got away with it?'

'Of course I do, silly. I was just teasing,' Lorna said.

'Thank you for doing this,' Claire said, reaching for her friend's hand and giving it a squeeze.

'Do you really think I wouldn't do everything I could to give my truest friend the wedding she always dreamed of?' Lorna said, raising an eyebrow. 'Especially after everything you did to make mine come true.'

Lorna winced and in that moment Claire forgot all about the secret wedding, the fear that someone would spill the beans and that the press would somehow manage to gatecrash.

'Are you all right?' Claire took Lorna's hands and guided her to a chair.

'I'm fine, Claire,' Lorna said, her face suddenly beaming. 'The baby kicked!'

Lorna guided Claire's hand to a point on her ever growing bump. Claire's eyes went wide.

'The baby kicked,' Claire whispered back. And then they were both crying and laughing all at the same time.

'You can't cry!' Lorna yelped. 'Your makeup!' Lorna was back on her feet reaching for a tissue before she gently wiped the tears that were forming in Claire's beautifully made up eyes.

There was a knock at the door.

'Ladies, it's time.' Jack's voice floated through the door.

Lorna grabbed Claire's hand and gave it one last squeeze.

'Let's go,' Lorna said, 'to the much

awaited for, most secret wedding of the year.'

And now Claire did manage a smile.

Claire's dad stood waiting for her, outside the venue, with the biggest beam on his face Claire had ever seen.

'My darling, you look beautiful,' he said, pulling a handkerchief from his pocket to dab his eyes. Claire leaned up and kissed him on the cheek. They had had to keep the guest list impossibly small to pull this off but she knew that all the truly important people were with her on her special day.

Music filtered through the closed doors, the Wedding March.

'Ready?' Jack said and Claire nodded as Jack threw open the doors to the lounge of Lorna's parents' home. Inside, Claire could see each one of the 20 guests sitting in chairs in the space that had been cleared of all other furniture and decorated just as a church would have been. And then there was Gabe, standing at the front, with Henry at his side and the local minister who was waiting to marry them.

Claire and her dad walked up the very short aisle that had been formed between the short rows of congregation. Claire only had eyes for Gabe, standing waiting for her, dressed in his kilt, as she had requested.

A reminder of the day when she knew she had fallen completely and hopelessly in love with him.

It had been a journey to get here.

Their relationship had quickly become gossip mag fodder but they had ridden out every storm and now they were here. Gabe had managed to pull it off.

All either of them had wanted was a wedding day that was theirs. A day that they could share with those they loved, with no paparazzi, and Gabe had done it and it was perfect. Claire's father kissed her one last time as a single woman and gave her hand over to Gabe.

'Hello,' Gabe said, sounding just a little bit nervous.

'Hello,' Claire said back with a little

giggle and then they turned to the minister and made their vows. To have and to hold. For richer, for poorer. In sickness and in health. For better or worse.

We do hope that you have enjoyed reading this large print book.

Did you know that all of our titles are available for purchase?

We publish a wide range of high quality large print books including:
Romances, Mysteries, Classics
General Fiction
Non Fiction and Westerns

Special interest titles available in large print are:
The Little Oxford Dictionary
Music Book, Song Book
Hymn Book, Service Book

Also available from us courtesy of Oxford University Press:
Young Readers' Dictionary
(large print edition)
Young Readers' Thesaurus
(large print edition)

For further information or a free brochure, please contact us at:
Ulverscroft Large Print Books Ltd.,
The Green, Bradgate Road, Anstey,
Leicester, LE7 7FU, England.
Tel: (00 44) 0116 236 4325
Fax: (00 44) 0116 234 0205

WILD SPIRIT

Dawn Knox

It's Rae's dream to sail away across oceans on her family's boat, the *Wild Spirit* — but in 1939 the world is once again plunged into conflict, and her travel plans must be postponed. When Hitler's forces trap the Allies on the beaches of Dunkirk, Rae sails with a fleet of volunteer ships to attempt the impossible and rescue the desperate servicemen. However, her bravery places more lives than her own in jeopardy — including that of Jamie MacKenzie, the man she's known and loved for years . . .